Waypoint Alaska

Always suk adventure!
Shauna R Schober
1/23/13

Copyright © 2011 Shauna R. Schober
Edited by Stephanie Curry & Laura Estes
Cover design or artwork by Josh Jones

All rights reserved.

ISBN: 1-4637-1672-9
ISBN-13: 9781463716721

Waypoint Alaska

Shauna R. Schober
Edited by Stephanie Curry & Laura Estes
Cover design or artwork by Josh Jones

2011

Dedication

For Faith Ann Fulmer, aka: the Warrior Princess,

You've inspired me in ways you will never know, you are amazing and strong, brilliant and hilarious. You make me laugh, smile and pray, every day, and I am so grateful that I have the opportunity of knowing you.

⁂

Special thanks to Mrs. Anderson's third grade class at Oak Grove Elementary School, in Medford, OR. After reading Waypoint in class, these students chose the location for the third book in the Waypoint Book Series. Dennise B, Asher B, Paighton B, Janessa C, Addison C, Isabella C, Jesus C, Gustavo D, Ethan F, Kai F, Naomi H, Joel I, Juliet L, Caitlyn M, Lucero M, Jasmine N, Monica P, Angela P, Chayce P, Andre R, Jaccob R, Lanie R, Felipe R, Sophia S, Emily T, Christopher T, Johnny T, Yanet V, Sandra V, and Tanner W., I greatly appreciate your help and enthusiasm!

⁂

A big thank you to Karen and Steve for collecting maps and research material for this book, all my friends, family and fans, you are all amazing! Stephanie, Laura, and Josh, thank you so much for your hard work, I really couldn't do this without you guys. A special thank you, to Paul, for sharing Waypoint with so many of your friends and family, you rock! And as always thank you so much to my wonderful husband, David, for supporting me through this journey.

While the characters in this book are based on actual people, and the locations in this book do exist, this is purely a work of fiction.

The waypoints used do not lead to actual geocaches.

I

Thump, thump, thump...Ben's heart pounded in his ears... thump, thump, thump...it was getting faster. He thought it might explode, suddenly his arms took over and a loud crack filled the air. The impact of the ball hitting his bat shook his body, as he twisted and followed through he lost site of the flying orb...always a good sign he thought.

He ran, as fast as he could; screams, clapping, whoops and hollers following him around the bases, his foot hit first. He shot off of the base in no time; he was closing in on second. Again he launched himself past, approaching third now. A loud noise rang out in the distance. *What was that?* He ignored it as he flew past third; finally he was closing in on home, just a few more steps. He could see the pitcher's arm moving through the air, the ball was coming toward the catcher, he dove to the ground, dust in his face, filling his mouth, sliding as if on butter, finally his fingers barely hit the edge of home plate. The crowd went wild as the ump yelled, "SAFE!"

Again a noise echoed through the ball park, it was louder now, everyone in the stands was looking around, curiosity taking over, was it a song? No, no it had to be...an obnoxious vehicle horn. Ben twisted his head and then he saw it. In the parking lot was the biggest, ugliest, most dilapidated RV he had ever seen. It was painted camouflage, with what he guessed was spray paint. One headlight was actually hanging off the front of the beast, the horn sounded again, and then suddenly Ben's worst nightmare came true.

The door popped open, and suddenly he heard his name being called over the stands. Was she really doing this? *Really?* Ben flushed with embarrassment and ran, faster than he had circled the bases. Again his name was yelled. He hopped the cyclone fence, making "shut up" hand gestures the entire way.

"Hey buddy! So you like it? Huh, do ya?" Aunt Lacey hung out of the side door. She was so proud, not just of the fact that she had just humiliated her nephew, but also because she was actually proud of this monster. "Yep, I got her on sale, only paid fifteen hundred dollars for her." She patted the side of the RV gently as if loving on a small dog. As she did flakes of paint drifted to the ground.

"Why?" Ben asked. "Why do you have this? Why are you here?" he asked through clenched teeth.

"Oh you mean besides to see your face turn three shades of red?" she waved to the crowd of people who were turned around in their seats in the stands, "Nothing to see here people, go about your business" she yelled in a joking authoritative voice. Ben rubbed his forehead. He couldn't help but laugh.

He and Aunt Lacey had a friendship like no other, the previous summer the two had been involved in one of the craziest, scariest adventures of both their lives. Searching for a supposed prize of ten thousand dollars, going from one insane location to the next, it was the most bizarre and best experience of Ben's life. They must have driven over a thousand miles in the few days they were on that scavenger hunt, Ben thought.

"The reason, young lad, that I bring this marvelous vehicle to you is that we're not flying to Alaska." She interrupted his thought.

"What? Why not?"

Lacey tugged on some small beaded braids in her hair and pulled them into a pony tail to keep them out of her face. "Ben, it has been brought to my attention, that the only real way to explore Alaska is to travel the highway, the Alaskan Highway." She said this with a strange expression on her face, as if she knew of a secret or the punch line to a joke that Ben wasn't privy to yet.

"Okay, what's the big deal with that?" Ben asked.

"Oh young Ben," She stepped off the wobbly stairs of the RV. "The big deal is this!" she pulled a long bumper sticker out of her back pocket and handed it to him.

"I TRAVELED THE ALASKAN HIGHWAY AND SURVIVED," Ben looked confused. "I take it there is something special about this highway?"

A throaty laugh echoed out of her mouth, "I guess we'll find out," She smirked. "Hey guys!" she called over to Ben's little sister, Megan, and Ben's Mom and Dad, as they approached. "So what do you think?" she asked proudly.

They all stood in shock, Ben's parents knew better than to show Lacey the slightest bit of embarrassment, she thrived on being a colossal pain in the rear end.

"It's a beauty." Ben's dad said with a straight face.

"Wow, where did you get this castle?" Ben's mom asked mockingly to her sister.

"Shut up!" Lacey said in a defensive tone. "This castle is taking your son and daughter to Alaska with me."

Ben's mom laughed…she knew Ben and his aunt had been planning this trip for a year now, ever since they had won the million dollars through their last adventure, but she was nervous, especially knowing that this year Megan would be going with them.

"I got it for fifteen hundred dollars! I know! I know, super deal, and it even came fully decorated," she opened the door wider, inviting them into the RV.

As they entered each gasped as they looked at their surroundings. On one wall hung an old taxidermy deer head, it was covered in dust and cob webs, the old bright orange Formica counter tops were chipped and stained, holes in the sofa released foam and fuzz onto the floor, the seats in the cabin of the RV were cracked and faded from years of sitting in the sun. All of this was overwhelming, and frankly a little scary, but the worst part was the smell. A combination of rotten eggs, and perhaps, was it skunk? Yes skunk, filled the air.

"It reeks in here, Aunt Lacey," Megan announced.

"Yeah, that's the only thing about this that sucks," Lacey responded.

"The only thing?" Ben's mom and dad laughed as they eyed each other.

"But old Betsy here will take us to Alaska in style," Lacey gently patted a stuffed squirrel which was mounted to the counter behind the sink. "She's authentic, I mean look we have our own squirrel here! Yep, I think Betsy is the perfect vehicle for this adventure. You can't go to Alaska in something beautiful, certainly not on the Alaskan Highway, I've heard stories, we need something rustic, something that has already been proven to last the test of time. Something that can handle a few dings."

Ben looked at his parents wide eyed, "well it is official, Aunt Lacey has gone totally insane."

"What? How have I gone insane?" Lacey interjected.

"Aunt Lacey, Garmin and United Cellular are paying for this trip, it's part of my advertising contract, we should be flying, high-class in style!" Ben argued.

"Let me tell you something young man," Lacey slammed the exterior door to the RV so no one outside could hear them, as soon as it slammed, the door fell off its hinges and crashed to the ground. She jumped in fear, "Anyways." she shook her head ignoring her embarrassment. "Just because we have the money and someone else is footing the bill for this trip doesn't mean we waste it! And like I said before, we are going to Alaska for an adventure, sheesh Ben, we aren't just tourists!"

Megan raised her hand as if she were sitting in class, "Um, yeah...we kinda are," she argued.

"I refuse to be a tourist, from now on we are all *'travelers'!*"

Megan rolled her eyes and sighed, "uh huh, whatever Aunt Lacey, just don't make me wear a fanny pack."

※

"Are we there yet?" Megan asked from the small dinette table in the living area of the RV.

Lacey threw the GPS unit to her.

"Not even close! Geeze, we've been on the road for like over two days!" she whined.

"Yes...it's been quality time for me too, Megz." Lacey said sarcastically. "I'll wake you up when we get close, we still have over two hundred miles," she reassured her.

Megan stood up, and disassembled the kitchen dinette table she was sitting at, it folded into a small bed, she plopped down, put her ear buds in and dosed off to sleep.

※

The RV sputtered and swayed up the highway. If it weren't for the constant road noise, curves, gravel, and broken asphalt, Lacey would have fallen asleep ages ago, but the Alaskan Highway was acting as great stimuli. It was hard enough steering the huge RV on normal roads, but this was definitely more of a challenge.

She embraced this though. This trip would prove to her family that she was able to take care of the kids, have a normal vacation, and no potential police phone calls home, unlike her and Ben's adventure the previous summer. She shivered as she thought of all the harm they were in, suddenly Ben interrupted her thoughts,

"So this geocache were stopping at…listen to the clue again, what do you think it means? *'One in a million.'*"

"My guess is it's on a tree or something, ya know a *million trees*, we'll figure it out. Do you have those coordinates handy? Double check them on the areal map on your phone," Lacey instructed.

Ben pulled out his phone from United Cellular, it was part of the overall prize package he had won on his last adventure, the phone went with him everywhere, and he knew for this trip his parents were tracking it online, 'just in case' they had said, whatever that meant. He quickly read the coordinates aloud, "60 degrees 03'46.48"North, and 128 degrees 42'39.88"West, right?"

Lacey glanced at the sticky note that was attached to her visor, "yep, looks right." After a short second the phone vibrated with results.

"Huh?" Ben sighed.

"What? What's up?" She asked.

"Well they're not trees, I'm not sure what it is, some sort of strange dots or buildings or something next to the road, seems to go on for a long ways. Anyhow, the town's name is Watson Lake. Who placed this geocache?"

"Someone named Cache Master. Actually the only reason I chose this one was because of the guy's name…'Cache Master'… cool huh?" she replied.

"Uh, sure. So you picked this geocache solely on this guy's name?"

"Yep, I couldn't resist, anyone who could come up with that name, well I had to see what they would put into their geocache, they are the 'Cache Master' after all." she laughed to herself. Ben rolled his eyes and settled into his seat, they still had 170 miles before they would arrive in Watson Lake. Something told him he was going to need his rest.

※

Lacey brought the RV slowly to a stop alongside the road in Watson Lake, Canada. Her eyes couldn't quite understand what she was seeing. Along the side of the road there were hundreds, no maybe thousands of posts with street signs all over them, covering them from top to bottom. There had to be thousands of them, from what appeared to be every place in the world. She turned the key and listened as the RV sputtered and then died. Then she kicked Ben in the calf to wake him up. "Found out what 'one in a million' means," she gestured in front of them. Ben's eyes grew wide with amazement and anticipation.

"How will we find the right one?" He rubbed the sleep from his eyes trying to get a better focus on the masses and masses of sign ahead of them.

"Well, I'm guessing the GPS will bring us within a few feet, right? We'll find it." Lacey squeezed in the back section of the RV and gently woke Megan up. "We're here." Megan jumped, clearly not remembering where she was, then let out a little scream as the vision of her aunt standing underneath the massive taxidermy deer head came into focus. "Oh sorry babe, did I scare you?" Lacey asked.

"No the deer head, it just creeps me out."

"Yeah, this thing has a lot of character, doesn't it?" Lacey took her sunglasses off the top of her head and slid them on the deer's face. "There, problem solved, hard to be scared of him now, huh?" She patted the deer's fur, what seemed to be a century's worth of dust and deer hair wafted through the air. She quickly rubbed her hand on her pants as she made a disgusted face. "Eww...anyways, get up, let's go!"

Megan smiled as she slipped her shoes on, it was so exciting to be on this trip, last year she hadn't gotten to come, she was "too young" her mother had said, but this year she couldn't use that excuse. While everyone else hoped that the trip would be a simple vacation, she secretly hoped something amazing would happen, something crazy, outrageous, and maybe even a bit scary.

Ben slid through the space in the seats to the living area of the RV, "okay, I have my phone with the waypoint, we're only about fifty feet away. I was looking online, this place is called the 'Sign Post Forrest' people leave a sign with their home town, or state or country on one of the sign posts. There are tens of thousands here!" He was excited for the challenge, but almost felt disappointed, nothing exciting could happen in such a safe place, he thought. He quickly brushed off his disappointment and carefully opened the door. His dad had replaced the hinges, but he was still nervous of the dilapidated beast.

As they stepped out into the sunshine, there was a chill in the air. Even for June it was only 65 degrees here. They welcomed the breeze though, anything was better than the smell and stuffiness of the RV, which sadly they had almost gotten used to after being in it for almost three days. Towering above them and around them were hundreds of poles, all covered in signs of different colors. It was pretty impressive.

"I wanna put up a sign," Megan said.

"We don't have one, maybe next time," Lacey tried to appease her niece.

"Next time? Yeah right." Megan started walking around looking and touching the signs, it was pretty impressive after all. Each of these represented a person, or family who had traveled this same road, they had seen the same mountains, maybe the same wildlife, they had felt the bumps in the road, they had been here in this exact spot and decided that their journey was so special they should leave a sign, a memento stating that at some time they were here in this exact spot. Megan felt a bit emotional about this revelation when all the sudden a shout echoed in her ears.

"Found it!" Ben's voice boomed. He was standing in front of a tall post, phone in hand, "Look right above that sign from Melbourne." Lacey and Megan headed toward him and looked up to where he was pointing, sure enough six signs up was a sign that read "Cache Master."

"Well that wasn't tough," Lacey said, elbowing Ben.

"Yeah that was super easy, but uh...where's the cache?" Ben asked.

"Well let's look around here, it's gotta be close, the waypoint leads here." Lacey began looking at the back of the post, on the ground, suddenly Megan said,

"Hey something's written on the back of the sign."

Ben looked closely, "okay it says *two left, three down, four up*," he sighed. "What does that mean?"

"Well let's think about this, '*two left*.'" Lacey looked at the front of the sign, then she looked to the left. She moved two posts to the left, "okay now three down." She looked at the top of the post and counted three signs down. "Okay, now four up. Wait, I can't go four up?"

"I can," Megan said. Lacey turned around, Megan was standing about five feet behind her, she pointed eagerly to something behind the post Lacey was standing in front of. "Check it out," Megan grinned.

Lacey moved to where Megan was standing and Ben followed, both focusing in on what Megan was pointing to. Behind the original post was another post, further back. It too was stacked with signs, but the very top one, the only one that showed from where they were standing read, "Wanna Play?"

"Sweet!" Ben ran to the post and began climbing the fence directly behind it, "I got something!" he hollered. He ripped something off the back of the sign and jumped off the fence just as Lacey and Megan approached. In his hand he held a zip lock bag with a small envelope inside, he opened the bag and slid the envelope out. On one side in very small calligraphy print read, "If you decide not to follow the instructions please replace this envelope exactly where you found it. Thank you, Cache Master." Ben opened the envelope and found a small brass key, and a note. He read, "If you're serious and wanna play my game, go to the waypoint on the enclosed key. I must warn you, this is not for the novice." He looked at Lacey and Megan, his mouth wide with awe.

"Well let's go!" Megan blurted as she jumped.

"Wait…we don't even know who this guy is? This was the only geocache he had listed on geocaching.com." Lacey's anxiety came through her words. "Plus, we are headed to Alaska, this key might not go to a cache in Alaska, it could lead anywhere."

"There's only one way to find out." Ben turned the key over and showed Lacey and Megan the inscription on the back, he then entered it into his phone. "58 degrees 26'18.04" North and 134 degrees 59'49.43" West." He then hit enter, a second later excitement overcame him, "How ya like me now?" he said as he shoved the phone in his aunt's face. Sure enough the red dot indicated the waypoint to be next to the ocean, on the coast of Alaska.

"I guess I can't argue with that, but are we sure?" Lacey looked sternly at both Megan and Ben, she so didn't want to get in trouble again.

"Of course we're sure," Megan said, "I mean, what could happen?"

Lacey chuckled nervously, she looked at Ben, hoping he would back her up and tell Megan no, tell her that anything could happen, tell her that they could get hurt, that they could die, that, that...Ben interrupted her thoughts,

"Best case scenario, we win a million dollars," he laughed, then immediately stopped as he read his aunt's expression. "Worst case scenario, we go, it's too dangerous, so we bail. Or we go, it's lame, and we find another cache on geocaching.com." Ben and Megan both stared at their aunt.

"You're right, you're right, I mean what are the odds of something crazy happening two years in a row, right?" Lacey shook her head, almost surprised that these words were coming out of her mouth, as she said them she felt it deep down inside, she knew it was a lie, she knew something wasn't right. She felt scared and panicked, but deeper down, under all that fear, she really did, *wanna play.*

2

Ben stretched his arms high as he climbed out of the taxi cab that had brought them through the Alaskan capital city of Juneau. The air was crisp, and cool, but the sunshine was unbelievable, it was shining almost twenty hours a day, bright, clear, and sort of exhausting. His body still hadn't grown accustomed to not having a dark night which forced him to sleep. After days of riding in the RV, and then another trip on the Ferry boat over to Juneau, the lack of sleep was really starting to wear on him. Perhaps he could convince Aunt Lacey to stay in Juneau for the night so they could all get a good, "RV free" night sleep.

Megan stood next to Ben staring at the blue waters of the ocean in front of them, she almost seemed annoyed when Aunt Lacey suggested they get their bearings before starting to look for the cache. Already, this trip has started slow. After all the driving, then riding on the boat, while fun, it wasn't exactly what Megan thought an adventure should consist of.

"Okay so Ben, let's look at the map on your phone now that we are here, where is the exact waypoint?" Lacey insisted. Ben pulled his phone from his jacket pocket, and advanced past his text message screen to the aerial map of their location. He zoomed in to get a closer look.

"Huh," he said. "Well it looks like we were a little off with this waypoint."

"What do you mean 'a little off'?" Megan questioned.

"Well...the dot on my screen...it's um, in the water, like way in the water," he paused. "I think the geocache, might be out there," he stretched his arm in the direction of the frigid sea.

Lacey sighed, "Great," she huffed. Ben continued to play with his phone.

"Okay, I double checked and yes, this waypoint is right, but...look at this." He passed the phone to Megan who then shoved it in Lacey's face.

"Is that what I think it is?" Lacey questioned.

Ben grabbed her shoulder, spun her to the right and pointed, eagerly. In the distance she saw an enormous cross that stood out of the jagged rocks which bordered that side of the beach. Lacey instinctively started walking, Ben and Megan followed. "Where are we going?" Megan asked.

"I wanna be sure about this, maybe the coordinates were off? Maybe the geocache is by the cross, and not, well in the actual water" Lacey tried to think as fast as she could. What would she tell them if Ben was right and they had to go into the water. She would definitely make them get scuba equipment, she knew the kids had gone scuba diving in Hawaii, but that was only for one day, could they do it in this cold water? Could she?

They finally reached the cross, after slipping and scraping knees on the rocks of the jagged reef. The cross stood a lot taller than any of them thought it would, it must have been about 15 feet high. They all looked around the base, found nothing, around the rocks, nothing, and then Lacey saw something. A small metal marker right at the junction of the two cross arms. She squinted to see it better, the salty sea air had corroded the metal, the letters were blending together in a mixture of greens and dark rusty colors, but finally she made out what it said. As she started reading

Ben and Megan froze, "In Honor of the 353 souls lost, voyaging on The Princess Sophia. Vanderbuilt Reef. 1918." Lacey shivered.

"So is Ben right? Is this a ship wreck? Will we be going down and exploring a sunken ship?" Megan asked.

"I think so, I think we need to get to a scuba store and rent some equipment, because if this isn't some crazy joke, then our geocache is sitting at the very bottom of the ocean." Lacey pointed as she motioned with her hand toward the sea. "You both ready for that?"

"Bring it on." Ben said.

"I've just been waiting for you to say, *Go!*" Megan added enthusiastically.

"So I'm the only one who's a little nervous about this?" Lacey questioned, Ben and Megan nodded their heads eagerly. "Great," she mumbled.

༺༻

An hour later the three climbed out of a tour van. It was a good thing, Lacey now realized, that they couldn't bring the RV through the town, the roads were too narrow and it would have been a night- mare trying to drive and park. But right now as she was deciding on where they should go to change into their dry suits and scuba equipment, she really wished they had the old RV for a dressing room.

The tour guide answered her question when he pulled open the back doors of the van and strung a cord to hang a curtain on to make a semi private changing room. "We'll just get changed and the boat will come pick us up in a few minutes, one great thing about doing the 'Princess Sophia Shipwreck' tour with us is that you don't have to carry an air tank, we have hoses that you'll take down to the wreckage with you, it doubles as a safety harness, if you get lost or stuck, we've got you on a leash!" he laughed at his own joke, then quickly popped out of the curtain.

Ben walked in next, followed by Megan and then finally Lacey changed into her dry suit. The three stood on the dock, flippers in hand waiting with the tour guide for the scuba boat to come pick them up. Within minutes it arrived and they climbed on. It was a four hour boat trip to Vanderbuilt Reef. The captain explained how the ship had gone done, how it had hit the reef and become stranded. It sat stuck on the reef for many hours, rescue had come but the winds and jagged rocks prevented them from coming close enough to unload the passengers. Ultimately the captain had called off the rescue boats, for fear of causing damage to them. He was certain the hull of the ship could hold and last until the weather changed and larger ships could come. He had called off the smaller ships, sent them away because of the foul weather, but as the storm grew fiercer the ship sank, ultimately the captain was wrong, and all lives were lost.

The story gave Ben chills, even though they were surprisingly warm in their scuba gear, the thick neoprene didn't let in any cool air, and it also didn't let any of their body heat escape. The captain of the boat went over basic instructions. The masks they were wearing were a little different, they looked more like an astronauts helmet than a diving mask. They didn't connect to an individual oxygen tank, just to a multitude of hoses that were bound together. Each hose delivered a different gas into the helmet, to create breathable air. And each hose could extend hundreds of feet down into the depths of the ocean from the scuba boat above.

They put on their flippers, large helmets and gloves. Before the captain connected their oxygen tubes he attached large glow sticks on each of their chests and backs, he called them his own little search and rescue identifiers. Just in case the worst happened. He assured them though, nothing would happen to them while under his watch. Once they were connected to their oxygen tubes he gave them each a thumbs up. Ben patted a small zippered pocket on his hip, just to reassure himself that he did in fact have the geocache key. It was so small and yet at this moment it felt heavy, the anticipation of what treasure the key could unlock made his heart beat faster. He felt a little more confident knowing that his aunt had the waterproof cell phone, which could receive GPS imagery even under water. It could also pinpoint the exact spot they needed to be in, just then his thoughts were interrupted when suddenly the distant sound of water brought him back to reality. He saw Megan roll backwards into the ocean and then his aunt followed. He said a quick prayer then turned and forced himself to fall backwards off the boat as well.

Once in the water the low hum and static of the microphones filled their helmets. Ben looked down toward his aunt and sister; they were kicking hard, swimming eagerly in order to be the first to reach the wreckage below. Suddenly, Ben was reminded of his near drowning experience in Crater Lake, his stomach turned for a moment and he froze, the panic overcame him. He tried to remember that he ended up fine, he was here now in this place, and right now he had to focus.

Lacey and Megan were now much deeper in the dark water, he could barely see the glow from the glow sticks that were attached to their chests. He mustered some courage and faced down getting ready to swim to them. "Hey guys, wait up," he said loudly into his helmet, the radio would carry the sound to both his sister and aunt. He was surprised that they didn't turn, they didn't respond, did they even hear him? Just as he was about to say something else to try to get their attention something grabbed his shoulder, the weight pushed him down, he panicked and struggled, thrashing about. Suddenly he felt both shoulders being commanded down, something was pushing on him, he continued to fight. Trying to throw punches and prevent his attacker from gaining control, but in his panic his helmet fogged up, he couldn't see anything, he was breathing too heavily. Suddenly his chest felt tight, he realized he couldn't breathe, his eyes got blurry, he tried to kick his assailant, but somewhere in the middle of lifting his leg, trying to get enough strength and fighting the resistance of his flipper in the water, Ben passed out. His head rolled to the front of his helmet, unconscious, his body went limp. He floated in the water for a brief moment, and then suddenly disappeared.

Lacey and Megan pulled themselves deeper into the water. It was so dark that even with the aid of their underwater flashlights they could only see ten feet in front of them. Hundreds of fish zoomed around them, first scared and then slowly becoming more aggressive in their movements. The pressure of the water felt strange on their bodies, and the silence was eerie.

As they continued down into the depths of the ocean Lacey noticed what appeared to be a cloud of white below them, she turned to point it out to Ben. But all she saw was blackness. Frantically she spun, looking for him, where was he? Wasn't he right behind them? She turned to Megan and gasped "Where's Ben?" Megan also spun, shining her light in every direction.

"He was right behind us? Where'd he go?" Megan panicked.

"No clue! We better head back up to the boat, maybe something happened." She started pulling herself through the water and suddenly it wasn't Megan's voice echoing in her helmet.

"Lacey?" A man's voice called out.

"Yes? Who is this?" She demanded as she looked to Megan for answers.

"It doesn't matter, who this is. All that matters is that you have something I want and I have something you want, or should I say, someone."

"What?" She shrieked into her helmet, swimming faster toward the surface.

"Calm down Lacey, you can't come up too quickly now, don't wanna get the *bends*," he teased. "Now Lacey, let's think about this, what is more important? Don't you wanna see your nephew again?"

"Of course, now who are you, let me talk to Ben!" she begged now.

"Not gonna happen, I'll tell you what is gonna happen, though. You and your little friend are gonna go to that ship wreck and you're gonna find that safe. Once you do, you're gonna bring it to me."

"Safe? What safe?" she questioned.

"Don't play dumb girl! You know what I'm talking about!"

"I really don't and besides, I don't have the key, only..." she tried to negotiate with him.

"Don't you worry about that, I've got the key right here in my hand. Wasn't too hard to get away from Ben here, he couldn't put up much of a fight. So do as I say and your nephew lives, you have one hour. And Lacey, don't try anything funny, I've got my hand on your oxygen valve up here on the boat." He sighed heavily.

"What should we do?" Megan asked, tears running down her cheeks.

"I guess we have to go, and we have to remember that whoever this is they are listening to us." Lacey responded. Just as she finished her sentence the man's voice returned,

"I am listening, and I'm watching the clock, hurry up girls... time is running out."

3

Megan grabbed her aunt by the shoulders to try to get her to stop panicking. "Aunt Lacey, c'mon we just have to find it and bring it to him, or them or whoever. We'll just hand it over and then get Ben and be done with it. It's okay, I know it is, I can feel it."

Lacey shook harder, her sobbing was uncontrollable now, how had this happened again? She thought she had done everything right. She had chosen a simple geocache, and followed the clues, but somehow they had messed up along the way. Was this geocache special? What was in it? Why would someone take Ben to try to get it? Lacey wracked her brain for any reason this could be happening when suddenly she felt Megan pulling on her foot.

"What are you doing?" she growled.

"Well, you heard him, we are running out of time, we still have to make it down to the ship- wreck, find the geocache, and get it to the top!" Megan continued to pull, "And aunt Lacey, I'm guessing there is something special about this geocache, like maybe it's hard to get out of the shipwreck or something, why else would this guy take Ben? Why wouldn't he just come down and get it himself?" Finally Lacey began to swim next to Megan, kicking and pulling deeper into the dark water.

"Maybe this is all just a scam, ya know, like last time?" Lacey tried to convince herself.

"We won't know 'til we get to the top, c'mon," Megan encouraged her aunt.

As they moved deeper into the water the silhouette of the shipwreck came into view, it definitely didn't belong among the jagged rocks of the reef. The sleek lines of the bow seemed eerie in this setting, and although it wasn't moving and hadn't in almost one hundred years, it appeared to be alive. They swam closer and realized the movement was coming from the thousands of white sea anemones that had attached themselves to the metal and wood.

"Looks like cauliflower," Megan said as she shone her light on the waves of white. They swam harder and reached a jagged piece of steel that was sticking out of a large pile of rocks. Evidently it was these rocks that had brought the ship down. Megan looked to the sandy sea floor below her flippers. Aunt Lacey was busy pressing screen buttons on Ben's cell phone, it was still impressive to Megan that this phone was water proof, even when they were down so deep. Megan turned toward the ocean floor, looking at pieces of metal, a box that had been rusted almost all the way through, and even broken pieces of pottery that had never moved since their final fall from the ship. She glanced around some more and then she saw it. Shivers ran down her spine when she realized what she was looking at. About five feet in front of her wedged between two rocks was a an old leather boot. She swam over to it, and wiggled it free from the clenches of the reef rocks. A lump came to her throat when she realized this boot had belonged to one of the many passengers that had died when the ship sank. She tucked the boot under her arm and swam back to her aunt.

"Any luck?" she asked.

"Yep, I think we have to go about twenty feet this way," Lacey motioned in front of them, toward the massive ship. They looked at each other trying to gather enough courage to move closer. Together they advanced, methodically moving through the water. As they got closer to the side wall of the ship they moved with more deliberate motions, for some reason this place felt sacred, and they felt like intruders or trespassers. Indeed the ship deserved their respect.

Once they reached the rusted metal side they immediately realized a problem, there was no geocache, which meant it must be on top of or inside the shipwreck. They both continued to swim together, not wanting to lose sight of one another for even a second. They swam to the top of the side wall, over the ship's railing, looking for any entry point. The wooden planks were broken and awkward, more sea anemones clustered together, forming communities all over the railings, benches, and even the ships steering wheel. Megan explored the exterior of the cabin area while Lacey tried to lift the jagged pieces of wood that had once made up the flooring. Once they had both realized there was no geocache they decided to move to the other side of the ship. As they slowly floated toward the sea floor they saw the dark, ragged tear in the side of this ship. This was what had brought the ship down, this must have been where the reef rocks had torn into the Princess Sophia.

Megan swam faster, shining her light in all different directions and then slowly into the hole. She peeked first, building courage. The water was murkier inside, the particles that were floating in the water, shone brightly in the thick beam of her light. Lacey came to her side and placed her hand on Megan's shoulder.

"You ready? If you're too scared, I can..." she choked back on the fear in her throat, "I can go in, if you want, ya know, if you're too scared, I can go in by myself."

"No, we'll both go in," Megan watched her aunt's face relax as she reassured her. "We'll just need to be careful of our air hoses." They both looked at the long hoses that connected to the back of their helmets; this reminded them that they needed to hurry, in the surreal environment of the shipwreck they had almost forgotten that a dangerous man was on the other end of their oxygen hoses, literally holding their lives in his hands.

Lacey moved carefully through the hole in the side of the ship, she shone her light all over, making sure there wasn't anything hiding within the ancient walls. Megan followed, slowly maneuvering her air hose as she positioned herself toward the top of the room.

This must have been an engine room, she decided, as there were huge machines, with pipes that had corroded differently than the rest of the metal of the ship, these were a gorgeous green color, almost beautiful when the light hit them just so.

Lacey began looking around the edges of what she figured to be large engines, as she did small fish emerged, from their dark hiding places. They frightened her at first, but soon she felt at peace when she saw them, at least something was surviving in this devastation. Finding nothing she motioned to Megan to come closer.

"Do you see anything that could be the geocache?"

"Nope, there's a hallway through that opening though, do you wanna go into it, or should I?" Megan secretly hoped that Lacey would let her go, but didn't want to seem to eager. Lacey pulled the cell phone from the small zippered pocket on her dry suit.

"This phone is crazy, I can't believe it's still working," she said almost to herself. "Well, this says that we're in the perfect spot and the accuracy is within ten feet."

"Down here, ten feet is a lot, Aunt Lacey," Megan looked around, "hey, wait, look over there, behind that metal beam, there's a door." She pointed to a thick rusted orange piece of steel, it must have fallen from the ceiling, and was now resting diagonally across the front of one of the smaller engines. The small engine had what looked almost like an oven door, with a large lever to lock it shut.

They both moved closer. Lacey grabbed a hold of the steel beam and wiggled it, trying to move it away from the door. At first it wouldn't budge, but then, suddenly it became loose and began falling into her. Even in the water the beam was extremely heavy. She tried to push it away, but wasn't strong enough, its weight forced her to the floor, the beam, as if in slow motion continued its silent fall, and smashed into her helmet with a quiet thud. Suddenly a crack emerged in the glass in front of her eyes. She panicked, as she realized at any second the glass front of the helmet may shatter, leaving her breathless one hundred feet below the surface.

༄༅

Ben slowly opened his eyes, he was in terrible pain, and totally exhausted. The overcast skies created a glare, he could only see the feet of what appeared to be two men. Anytime he twisted his head to try and get a better look the glare made it impossible to see their faces. He recognized one of the voices; it was definitely the captain of the tour boat. Why was he here though, why wasn't he in the water?

"What happened?" he asked, his voice scratchy. Just moving his jaw to speak made his head pound louder.

"Oh, he's awake" he heard the captain say as the feet moved closer to him. Suddenly a hand was on his shoulder.

"So, you're awake now, huh?" The captain's face was right above him now. Ben knew something was wrong, just by the expression on this man's face.

"Why am I up here? Where's Lacey and Megan?"

"They're down at the shipwreck, they're okay, so far," he mumbled.

"What do you mean?" The captain pulled Ben up onto his knees, suddenly Ben realized his hands were tied behind his back.

He hadn't noticed at first, due to the bulkiness of his dry suit. He struggled for a second and then realized there was no use.

"Well, see, it all started when I saw you put this pretty little key in your pocket," he raised the key so Ben could see it. "It got me wondering, why would this kid have a key? And why would this kid be taking said key down to the shipwreck? All's I could come up with is that this must be *the key*."

"What do you mean *the key*?" Ben asked innocently.

"Oh don't play dumb with me boy, there's only one thing that's locked on that ship, and as far as anyone can guess it's the safe that has all the gold in it," he snorted, and rubbed his thick gray beard, "but you're gonna tell me, that you're bringing a key down to a shipwreck for something other than to unlock the safe?"

"Wait, wait. What safe?" Ben asked genuinely. "We're just geocaching, we don't know anything about gold? We barely know anything about this shipwreck!" he struggled a little, but soon realized there was no point in wasting his energy.

"He sounds pretty serious boss," the other man said, Ben looked to him and nodded.

"Seriously we're just looking for a geocache, we found that key at the last geocache, it had the waypoint inscribed on the back, so we came here. We didn't even know it was in a shipwreck until we saw the cross in Juneau," Ben sighed heavily.

"Well, we'll just have to wait and see what your aunt brings back to me. If this key opens what I think it will I'll be one happy man."

"What about us? What are you gonna do with us?" Ben asked.

"Well, let's just say this, don't you worry about not seeing the shipwreck, kiddo, shortly after your aunt brings me the safe, you'll all be swimming with the fishes."

4

Megan swam over to her aunt. Her face was pale, shock was taking over. She saw the thick crack in the face plate of Lacey's helmet, they didn't have much time. "Don't move" Megan instructed her. She then grabbed onto the thick steel beam and rolled it off of Lacey. As it landed on the ship's floor a cloud of dirt, sand and algae rose and filled the space.

Megan turned and moved through the murky water. She grabbed onto the lever of the engine door, wiggled it a bit, and then pulled as hard as she could. There was a sudden release and then the handle moved easily, she slowly pulled open the door, and peeked inside. She assumed this was once a coal burning engine, due to its oven-like appearance. Inside she could tell that someone had been in this boiler recently, it was a small space, only about five feet by five feet, it was rusted and covered with some sort of sludge, she assumed it to be oil or coal residue. She searched the inside of the space and then spotted something, there, floating in the back of the boiler was a small black box. It appeared to be made of thick plastic or rubber; she entered the boiler and slowly inched toward it. She peeked back to her aunt, she was sitting extremely still in the engine room, eyes wide with fear, she hadn't moved an inch.

Megan grabbed the box, it felt slippery with her neoprene gloves on, she looked at it for a brief moment, it didn't seem to be anything special, but it did have a small lock on the front, this must be the geocache, she thought. She tucked it under her arm, turned and swam out. "Okay Aunt Lacey, this must be it."

Lacey wanted to reach for the case, but was too terrified of her face mask shattering. Megan saw the terror in her eyes and realized Lacey was too afraid to even speak. "It's okay, we'll slowly head to the top." Lacey moved the slightest bit and suddenly small air bubbles started to form and creep out of the crack on her mask. She motioned for Megan to look. Megan saw the air bubbles and grabbed her aunt's hand, they had to get out of here. They continued to swim slowly around the ship, over the top, around all the bright white sea anemones, as they moved through the water, Lacey felt moisture start to enter her helmet, she again motioned for Megan to look, slowly drops of water were entering through the crack, any other change in pressure would surely shatter the mask. Quickly, Megan lifted her free hand and pulled her neoprene glove off. The icy water caused her hand to go into an instant cramp, she shrieked from the stabbing pain, but quickly regained her composer. Lacey watched as her niece removed the thick band that held a head lamp on her helmet, she handed the geocache to Lacey, then put the glove over the front of Lacey's mask, in an effort to temporarily seal the small holes in the crack. Once she had it in place, she carefully slipped the thick band around the top of Lacey's helmet and centered over the glove on the front of Lacey's mask.

Lacey floated in pure darkness, the only peace she had was that she felt no more water enter her mask. Megan pulled her through the water, pausing every few feet to ensure they didn't rise up too quickly and get "the bends." She had heard so many stories of people who swam to the surface too quickly, the pressure changes would make them violently ill, and once they made it to the surface if they didn't get treatment right away they could die. "We're almost there. When we get to the top I want you to just wait in the water." Lacey couldn't tell what Megan was planning but she knew that she couldn't ask, due to the eavesdropping kidnapper who was waiting in the boat above them.

Megan slowly pushed her aunt to the surface, and squeezed her arm tightly, trying to tell her to stay quiet. Lacey instantly felt the change as she pushed through the surface, and suddenly a calming sensation overcame her, she had survived. So far.

The oxygen hoses were becoming more limp in the water, Megan grabbed a hold of hers and made a big loop. She carried the case in one hand, the large loop of hose in the other and purposely swam under the boat to the opposite side of where the hoses dropped into the water. When she was about three feet from the surface she released the geocache, the trapped air made it rise suddenly to the surface.

Ben heard a loud gushing sound of water, suddenly both men who stood above him moved toward the sound, quickly he rolled up onto his knees and then stood, his hands were still behind his back, but he was quickly forming a plan, he looked around the boat into the water and noticed aunt Lacey floating in the water about thirty feet from the boat on the opposite side. Where was Megan? Suddenly his question was answered. Both men were leaning over the edge of the boat, reaching for the geocache, just as Ben moved toward them Megan shot up out of the water and swung a loop of her oxygen hose around one of the men's neck and pulled him down into the water. Ben knew they wouldn't have much time. Just as the first man went over the edge Ben charged the second man, nailing him hard in the lower back with his shoulder, knocking him into the water.

Both men flailed around in the water. Megan quickly swam circles around them, looping them in her oxygen hose. The only advantage she had right now was that the temperature of the water was making it almost impossible for the men to fight back. As she made one final loop she took her hand that didn't have the glove on it and unlatched the thick metal clasp that connected her helmet to the rest of her dry suit, she slipped her head out as water rushed in, then quickly let it drop. The oxygen continued to spray through the mask, pulling both men all around as they wrestled to free themselves from the thrashing hose.

Megan quickly popped to the surface, she squealed in pain as the icy water poured down into her dry suit, quickly she swam over to the floating geocache, grabbed it and returned to the boat. She threw it onboard then lifted herself up and over the edge. Her entire body screamed in pain. She felt as though she were being stabbed with a million knives as the freezing water circulated through her suit. The hand that had been ungloved for so long was bright purple, she moved it around, trying to increase the blood flow. Ben moved over to her, "Are you okay?" She didn't answer, but turned him around and wiggled the plastic zip tie that was being used to cuff him.

"Hang on," she instructed. She quickly looked around, then saw the hose and remembered that Lacey was still in the water, as well as the men. She grabbed Lacey's hose and started pulling her in, closer to the boat. She was now literally using the oxygen hose as a leash.

Lacey felt the tugging and realized she could take the glove and band off her face mask, she slipped them off and began swimming, trying to help Megan as she pulled her in to the boat. Once to the side, she grabbed onto the edge and pulled herself over. "Where are the bad guys?" Lacey asked, Megan motioned to the other side of the boat where the men were still splashing in the water trying to untangle themselves. Megan then went to the front of the boat and grabbed a knife she assumed was used for gutting fish. She ran back to Ben, and cut off the zip tie that was around his wrists.

"Okay Ben, where's the key?" Megan almost yelled, her adrenaline was running full force.

"Umm..." he turned and looked at the two men.

"Oh no," Megan sighed. She turned to Lacey, she was still taking her helmet off and undoing her gloves. "What should we do Aunt Lacey?" Lacey looked over the side of the boat,

"HEY!" She yelled, "HEY!" the two men stopped splashing for a moment. "You gonna give us that key?" Lacey asked.

"Y...you kidding? H...h...how stupid you think we are?" one of the men said as his full body shivers made him stutter.

"Well, pretty stupid I guess." Lacey turned and headed to the front of the boat, she started the motor, it roared to life, spraying the men. She looked back at them and nodded for Ben to ask again.

"You sure you don't wanna give it to us?" Ben asked.

"Wh..wh...why don't ya ja...jus...st come in and get it?" the man wailed again. Ben laughed.

"They said no, Aunt Lacey."

"Their choice, hold on guys." Lacey pushed the gear shifter into place and the front end of the boat lifted from the sudden inertia. All the sudden, the boat jumped and was speeding through the water. Ben and Megan held on tightly to the edge, watching the men being dragged by the oxygen hoses. They bounced along the wake. Every few seconds they could hear a muffled scream, and then it would be silenced by either the water or the sound of the motor. Suddenly the boat came to a stop. Lacey walked to the back of the boat,

"You sure you don't wanna give me that key?"

"O-O-OKAY!" one of the men screamed, the other seemed to be unconscious.

Lacey started to pull them closer to the boat. Ben grabbed the knife from Megan and held it defensively while the two men slowly and painfully climbed on the boat. They both collapsed as soon as they were out of the water.

"Okay, so where's the key?" Lacey demanded.

"He…heee….he's got it.." the man with the beard motioned to the other. Lacey leaned over the other man.

"Wait Aunt Lacey!" Ben yelled. It was too late though the other man had slipped his foot behind her leg and knocked her feet out from under her, she dropped to the floor with a thud. He quickly jumped on top of her and held her down. The other man stood up and started toward Ben and Megan. Ben pushed Megan behind him toward the steering wheel, then he whipped the knife up by his ear. The man continued to advance, more slowly now that Ben was raising the knife. Suddenly, Ben's hand whipped through the air, the man stepped to the side, clearly afraid of the knife flying at him. The knife flew through the air, end over end, and then finally it met its target as it stabbed the man holding Lacey in the hand. The knife went through his hand and literally pinned his hand to the floor of the boat. He screamed in pain and suddenly released his grip on Lacey to try to remove the knife. Lacey wiggled out from under her assailant, just as she grabbed the side of the boat, Megan threw the boat into gear. The instant speed threw the other man back onto the deck of the boat as well, and gave Lacey and Ben enough time to move closer to Megan.

They all looked at each other, not sure what to do, Ben grabbed the geocache off the floor of the boat and handed it to Lacey. "What next?" he asked.

"I'm thinking!" Lacey shrieked.

"Stop the boat!" a thunderous voice boomed over them. Megan turned in horror, Ben and Lacey stood leaning on the cabin of the boat with their hands up. Megan moved the shifter into neutral and slowly climbed out of her seat, a lump was growing in her throat. She turned and stared into the barrel of a large spear gun. The man who had fallen was pointing it directly at Megan, its sharp spear was only three feet from her face. She looked over to the other man, in one swift motion he pulled the knife out of his hand and the floor of the boat. Blood spurted from his wound, he quickly pulled his jacket off and twisted it around the wound. He took the knife in his good hand, and walked closer to Ben.

"Now boy, didn't I tell you what was gonna happen?" his words were still slurred from being in the freezing cold water and now the severe pain in his hand.

"Yeah," Ben sighed. He motioned for Lacey to hand him the geocache. Lacey passed it to him, her hands shook with fear. The man snatched it from her, he bit down on the knife to hold it in his mouth while he slipped his good hand into his pocket and retrieved the key. He slipped the key into the lock on the geocache. Lacey, Ben, and Megan all took a deep breath as the man opened the geocache. Inside were a black velvet liner, and another Ziploc bag. The man lifted the Ziploc bag out and hung it in front of Ben's face.

"What is this?" he looked to the man holding the spear gun. He put down the geocache box and opened the Ziploc bag; he slipped a piece of paper out, and then grabbed the brass key that was inside the bag as well.

"See," Ben interrupted the man, "it's just a geocache, not gold, I told you."

"Well, let's read this note first, boy." The bearded man unfolded the note, and read, *"Great work, I hope you're enjoying playing my game. If you choose not to go to the next geocache, please return this key and geocache to the exact spot you found it in. Thank you, Cache Master."* The man stared at the note, then eyed the key.

"See, I'm telling you man, this is not what you think," Ben insisted.

"Shut up, boy. I think I know exactly what this is. I think someone has moved the gold off that ship, that's the only thing that makes sense...Yeah, that's gotta be it. No one has ever found the gold from that ship wreck, over two million dollars' worth, and that was the value in 1918, imagine what it is worth today... Yep. I bet this key leads to the gold. What do you think?" he asked the man with the spear gun.

"I think you're right, only how do we know where to go?" he asked, genuinely confused.

"Oh that's easy," the other man said with a laugh. He motioned to Ben, Megan, and Lacey, "These guys are gonna take us there."

5

Ben and Megan stared at the back of their aunt's head. She was sitting in the seat in front of them in-between the two kidnappers. They had found out that the older one with the gray beard was named Henry, the younger one with the scratchy voice called himself Eddy. Megan had found out very early on that he was self-conscious of his full name when she purposely called him Edward. She sometimes had a knack for finding and pushing people's buttons. In this situation it could prove useful, she thought to herself.

The driver seemed to be an acquaintance of Eddy and Henry. He was a large man, very husky, with thick black hair, and a mustache that covered his entire mouth. His name was Jim. Although he did know Eddy and Henry, he didn't quite seem to understand what was so urgent, and why the pair was being accompanied by two children and a young woman. He played along though and did as he was told, being guaranteed along the way that he would be paid well for his help, and for keeping his mouth shut.

Megan pulled her strawberry blonde hair back into a tight pony tail, Jim looked at her in the rear view mirror, and she noticed that his dark eyes had a look of concern. "Help us," she mouthed the words to him so the kidnappers wouldn't hear her. Jim quickly put his attention back to the winding road, and glanced back to Megan every few moments. She felt as though he might be their only hope.

꩜

Jim pulled the van off the side of the road, in the distance a river could be seen, the thick green summer foliage had hidden it from view as they drove along the highway, but now Ben could see the water, and he could see something else. He blinked his eyes a few times, trying to decide if he was imagining this or not.

"Look at those," Megan gasped. She nudged Ben, even though he was already staring at the same spot of water through the branches.

They all climbed out of the van, Henry and Eddy stayed next to Lacey, and held on to Ben and Megan's shoulders once they had stepped out of the van. Jim circled around and stood next to his friends.

"Okay now Ben, you gonna tell us where to go?" Henry asked as he squeezed Ben's shoulder harder. "You told us to come up here, so now where?"

"I don't know. I'm just following the coordinates that were engraved on the key we found." Ben asked to see his cell phone, Jim had taken it to look at the map while he drove.

"Yeah," he passed the phone to Ben. " Sorry Henry, this is as close as I could get us, can't really drive in the river." Jim joked.

"What's that supposed to mean?" Henry complained as he stood next to Ben, looking over his shoulder.

Ben enlarged the map screen, "Well look, here are the coordinates, we got, 59 degrees 25'03.70" North and 135 degrees 55'48.02" West." He pointed to the screen, "That's right there, we are right here," he moved his finger a little bit to show where they needed to head. "So, we need to go toward the river." Ben turned and began walking. A heavy hand grabbed his shoulder.

"Wait a sec, give me the phone!" Henry barked at him. Ben handed him the phone casually. He was scared, but wasn't too worried, he knew that once he didn't check in with his parents they would start tracking the phone, sooner or later the police would be following the signal and they would be found. He continued walking toward the river, truthfully he was curious about what he and Megan had seen.

The group stepped onto the gravel pathway and headed down an embankment to the river's edge, the river gurgled and swirled around rocks and logs, and something in the air buzzed. Ben turned to acknowledge how awesome this was to his aunt and sister, he turned again and took in this view. In front of him, spread across the river, perched on the exposed rocks and pieces of logs, and flying through the air were hundreds of Bald Eagles. The sky was filled, they reminded Ben of the seagulls at the beach, how they would flock and fly in swarms when someone would feed them. This was the same, except they were enormous eagles. A shiver ran down Ben's spine, he recalled his adventure with the Bald Eagle in Oregon, the fear, the excitement and the ultimate reward. He wondered if this time he would be rescued again by this amazing animal.

"Well, let's get this show on the road." Henry snapped his fingers toward Ben. He lifted Ben's phone up to show Ben the screen.

"Okay, we need to go about fifteen feet into the water," Ben directed.

Henry laughed, Eddy began to walk forward toward Ben until Henry pulled him back. "Not gonna happen there Ben, you go into the water, you get the safe or geocache, whatever you say it is. Then you bring it to us. Ben turned and looked at the water once again, he would be walking by and disturbing at least twenty eagles in order to get to the proper location. He looked back to Henry, who forcefully grabbed onto Megan's ponytail, yanking her head backwards to his beard. "C'mon Ben, let's go!" He growled.

That was enough to make Ben hustle, he took one step into the water, he jumped from the cold as it penetrated his tennis shoe. The eagles started to notice him, they were so preoccupied with catching salmon that they hadn't really considered this group of people as a threat, until now that is. Ben took another step, and another, the rocks were slippery, the cold water now went up to his knees. In the distance he saw a pointed rock, one that didn't seem to belong in a river, it certainly hadn't been there long. It wasn't smooth like the others, it hadn't been worn down by the water, he thought. On this rock, three eagles were perched. Ben thought for a minute and then kneeled down, he grabbed a small pebble from the river floor and tossed it into the air toward the eagles. Suddenly, at least twenty eagles swarmed and tried to grab the rock in midair. Ben ducked in fear, as they swooped toward his head and screeched in loud disappointment. He continued to walk carefully toward the pointy stone, it was now only five feet away. He balanced as he got closer, the water was much higher now and insanely cold, but he knew he had to get this geocache. Hopefully it would prove to Henry that this was all just a big mistake, there was no gold, nothing, it was just geocaching.

Ben approached the stone, one eagle had landed and was perched, eyeing him curiously, "Shoo," Ben waved his hand at the giant bird. It looked at him as if he were an alien. He took one more step and was right next to the stone, the eagle finally raised its wings and took off into the air, clearly upset that his prime fishing spot was being overtaken by this alien boy.

Ben knelt down and searched around the stone, he saw nothing. He moved the river rocks that surrounded the large sharp rock, still finding nothing. Then, he decided he would move the large stone. He pushed as hard as he could, suddenly the rock popped out of the thick muddy sand. Through the water Ben could see something shiny. It was brass. He reached down into the mud as fast as he could, the cold water bit into his skin, the pain shot through his body and gave him an instant headache. He grabbed the key as quickly as possible, pulled it up, and looked at it thoughtfully.

Once again, the brass key was engraved with a waypoint. He held it up into the air. "Okay, I've got it!" he called. He noticed a commotion in the sky above his head. The eagles- not only were they upset about an intruder in their river, but now hundreds of bright white heads where directed at Ben's hand. He looked around, panic and fear, pounded through his body. "Why don't you let Lacey and Megan go, then I'll give you the key and you can head to the next geocache. We'll stop looking, you can have whatever it is this guy is hiding, okay?" Ben yelled over the screeching eagles.

"No, I think, you better stick with us, you seem to be good at this kid, just toss me the key, c'mon now." Henry tugged on Megan's ponytail causing her to yelp in pain. The eagles heard her yelp and focused on Henry for a moment. As the eagles moved closer to him and swarmed in the sky over Ben's head, Henry became a little nervous, "Okay Ben, let's get on out of here, just toss it here now, okay, just toss it here," he repeated the words trying to calm himself down.

Ben looked at the key once again, "If you say so," he said as he tossed the key toward Henry. In that moment Ben yelled, "Heads!" Lacey and Megan ducked and curled to the ground as quickly as they could. Henry, Eddy, and Jim all kept their eyes on the key, floating through the air until suddenly, hundreds of eagles were flying right toward them. As the brass key reflected in the sunlight, the eagles instinctively thought it was a fish. They dove, they screeched, their claws fought for the key in the air. The sky filled with the huge beasts, it seemed as if every eagle on that stretch of river was now headed directly toward the three men.

Megan and Lacey took their chance and ran toward the water. As they jumped in, screamed from the cold and headed toward Ben. The eagles continued to fight, midair over the key. Henry yelled as he dove onto the sandy beach trying to protect himself from the onslaught of angry, hungry eagles that were dive bombing him, but then suddenly it was quiet.

He looked up, the swarm of eagles was dissipating, and Eddy and Jim were in the fetal position on the beach next to him, covering their heads. He looked into the river, saw Ben, Megan and Lacey fighting the current as they ran to reach the shore on the other side of the river, and then he realized, the key was gone. He looked to the sky, hundreds of birds were flying in circles, looking again for places to roost, while they waited for the perfect catch, but one eagle he noticed was flying away, as it circled toward the road he saw the glimmer of the sun reflect off of something in its talons. It was something small, but the glare of sunlight made it painfully obvious to Henry, this was the eagle that had won the fight.

He turned to see Eddy and Jim still lying on the beach, he then noticed that the ground, the bushes, and trees, and especially the three of them were covered in a thick, slimy mess of white and green goo. He wiped it off his forehead, and cursed as he made the connection and realized that they weren't covered in goo at all, but rather the poop of at least one hundred eagles.

6

Lacey, Megan, and Ben ran as fast as they could, their clothes were soaked, water sloshed from their shoes, they leaped over rocks, ran through bushes and branches scratched their arms and faces as they tried to get as far away from the river as possible. After a good ten minutes, Lacey slowed down to look behind them. She motioned for Ben and Megan to slow and to be quiet to listen. Hearing nothing she sank down to the ground to try to rest. Ben and Megan dropped to the ground also, both panting in sheer exhaustion.

"Well, that was amazing! Good thinking throwing the key, Ben!" She patted him on the back.

"Yeah. Except now we don't have the key for the next geocache," Megan sighed, she wasn't quite ready for this adventure to be over yet. Ben saw the disappointment in her eyes, and then broke a small twig off one of the bushes next to them. He cleared a small area on the ground, of all grasses and pebbles, and then took the twig and started writing something.

"No worries, Megz," he motioned for her to look. There on the forest floor were two sets of numbers.

"58 degrees 33' 15.54" North and 155 degrees 47' 32.36" West. Ben you are a rock star!" Megan squealed as she jumped and hugged her brother.

"Shhhh!" Lacey shushed her as she fearfully looked around. "Seriously though, we don't have the key to unlock the next geocache, and well, guys this is getting really dangerous." She dropped her head to her knees and sighed loudly. "Are we really doing this?"

"Well Henry and Eddy don't have a clue where we're going, they never saw the key, as far as they know we're gone now too." Ben smiled a sneaky smile, "The only problem I see, Aunt Lacey, is that we don't have a GPS unit now, Henry has my phone."

"It also means that when Mom and Dad start to freak out and can't get a hold of us, they will start tracking your phone and it will lead the police to Henry and Eddy, then they'll be arrested! See, Aunt Lacey, nothing to worry about!" Megan beamed with excitement.

"Yeah except, we'll be missing! We can't *not* tell your parents where we're going." Suddenly she lifted her head, "Okay, so we'll call your parents as soon as we get back to the RV. We won't wanna give them all the details, they'd of course make us come home, but we'll let them know that we're all fine."

Ben and Megan smiled, then lifted their knuckles and bumped them together, Lacey lifted her hand and bumped knuckles too. But, all too suddenly the sound of a car interrupted the moment. They quickly jumped to the ground, just in case it was Henry. The car proceeded by, but this gave Ben a good idea. He carefully got up, motioned for Lacey and Megan to follow him. Slowly they looked around and then made their way to the road.

"If you're lost, always find a road and follow it, its got to lead somewhere" Ben said proudly.

"Wow, Ben, your Bear Grylls obsession is paying off!" Megan joked. They followed the road for some time, finally ending up at the main road that went along the Chilkat River, from here they knew to head into Haines, which was the closest town.

"Ya know, Haines is actually really close to where we boarded the ferry boat to get to Juneau, I bet we can get a shuttle or something to take us back to the docks where we parked" Lacey picked up her pace to catch up with Ben and Megan.

☙❧

Waypoint Alaska

Lacey bent down and reached her hand under the wheel well, right above the front driver's side tire of the RV, she retrieved a magnetic key box, she slid the small black box open and pulled out the spare key to the RV.

"I never thought I would be happy to see this thing again," Megan groaned, but then she brightened, "But I so am!"

"No kidding, home sweet *redonculous* home!" Ben joked as he waited for Lacey to unlock the door. Once inside, he grabbed a pen and paper and wrote the coordinates down again. He had been repeating them in his head the entire day. He smiled as he lifted the paper up and handed it to Lacey, she dug around in the glove compartment looking for her phone. They had stowed both her's and Megan's phones while going to Juneau, no reason to bring three along they had rationalized. And it ended up being a good thing, had they taken them Henry would have all three. Lacey turned her cell phone on, it vibrated to life, and then started dinging repeatedly as it announced all of her missed text messages and voice mails.

"This could take a minute," Lacey apologized. A few minutes later she entered the waypoint Ben had given her into her phone's map feature. "Looks like we're headed to Katmai National Park," she called to the back of the RV. There was no answer so she peered behind the seat; both Ben and Megan were sound asleep, one on the fold out chair and the other on the converted dinette table. "Well, I suppose *I'll* drive," she joked, she then looked closer at her phone's screen, "Correction, I'll drive *forever*, evidently. Dang Alaska is like *huge!*" She groaned. Lacey slipped her key into the ignition, buckled her seat belt and started the RV.

❧❦

The small plane bobbed and swayed as it flew below the thick clouds. Megan sat up front next to the pilot and Lacey and

Ben sat in the second row of seats. The seaplane could only seat a maximum of eight people. As Ben looked around he thought even then it would be a very tight squeeze. Luckily, today it was just the three of them and the pilot, Trent, who was about twenty-five, Ben thought. He was a nice guy, very talkative, a natural tour guide. As they approached a large lake he instructed the trio to hang on, he was bringing this bird down.

The seaplane glided down onto the water and came to a resting float in the middle of the lake. Ben had never experienced landing on water before, it was exhilarating and if he was honest, crazy scary! Trent got the plane anchored to the dock by the shore and then helped Ben, Megan, and Lacey out and onto the dock. They all pulled on a back pack, complete with bug spray, and what Trent referred to as "bear spray." Ben was not confident in the small can of liquid, especially when he stepped off the dock onto the soft muddy ground and saw one of what seemed to be hundreds of huge bear prints. They were easily ten inches wide, and the markings left by their claws were even scarier. The claws on some of the prints seemed to stretch a good five inches in front of each toe, he shivered with fear.

"Okay, so we have our packs, get your cameras ready, and we're just gonna go over a few more things before we head to the viewing platform." Trent lifted his pack onto his shoulders and adjusted a holster on his hip that was carrying bear spray on one side and a gun on the other. "So, a few things about where we're going; we want to be quiet, move slowly, no surprising these guys, okay? Also if a bear does start approaching you, don't run, they can run forty miles per hour, so believe me, you'll lose." Ben laughed quietly. "We've all got bear spray, obviously only use it if you have to, remember we are in the bears' home, and they are letting us watch and take pictures and most importantly, they aren't eating us for lunch, so let's be respectful." With that, Trent turned and started to slowly hike up the trail. Lacey checked the GPS on her phone, they were heading in the right direction, she hoped they wouldn't have to venture too far off the trail to find the geocache.

"Uh Trent, is there a bathroom along the trail at all?" Ben asked.

"No, sorry man, you can use a bush, or hold it."

"I'll hold it for now." Ben said as he continued to hike the path.

As they walked, they all took pictures of the beautiful landscape, the mountains in the backdrop, the tall grasses along the trail, and bear prints, hundreds of bear prints, that never ceased being amazing, especially to Megan, who took pictures of huge prints, medium prints and small baby bear prints. When she asked Trent about these prints, he reminded them never to approach or bother a mother bear and her cubs. At this time of year the new cubs would only be a few months old, they would be very curious as well, so any visitor had to be careful and make sure the mother bears didn't mistake them for threats.

Lacey looked at the screen of her phone then showed Megan and Ben they were close, very close. The group came over one last small knoll on the trail and there below them was the river, its water was loud, large rocks penetrated the surface. It swirled and gushed, and poured over a water fall in the distance.

"This is Brooks Falls," Trent informed them. "Just up ahead you'll see a small platform, it's perched right at the top of the falls, perfect for watching the bears catch fish. You guys'll love this!" he was getting so excited, Ben was impressed, this man had probably seen this a thousand times, he knew it like the back of his hand, it wasn't anything new to him and yet he was visibly excited, thrilled even, to be here. As Ben looked around and took in the multitude of bears feasting in the water, he instantly understood. A combination of excitement, fear, and awe filled him. The group walked to the platform quietly. Megan continued to take pictures. In the water in front of the platform were five different full grown bears, one of which was enormous. There were four other large bears, each very different in appearance, one was so light colored it almost looked like a polar bear.

"Is that a polar bear?" Megan asked Trent.

"No, those are more in the Northern part of Alaska, that is just a blonde colored brown bear, they can be all sorts of different colors, amazing huh?" he responded.

"Crazy," Megan concurred.

Ben and Lacey looked around the platform, it was hard to concentrate with the bears in front of them feasting on the fish. It was incredible to watch them and both Ben and Lacey caught themselves in a trance watching the different bears stand perfectly poised and ready just waiting for a fish to jump up the falls. Once the fish was in the air, the bear would simply move its head and catch the fish, it seemed so easy, and yet as Ben watched a smaller bear, clearly a cub, maybe a yearling, try to catch fish, he knew instantly it was not as easy as the older bears made it look. This bear was fumbling and slipping. Clearly frustrated, it moved closer to the larger blonde colored bear and attempted to steal the remains of fish that the older bear had caught. The larger bear gave a warning growl to the smaller bear, whose ears instantly perked up.

"That small one is named Cinnamon, his mom is the one who is growling at him, her name is Sugar. I named them." Trent said proudly. "Cinnamon is a riot, super clumsy, and very social, no matter how many times he gets growled at and bossed around by the other bears, he keeps trying. He's fun to watch."

"Do you name them all?" Megan asked.

"No, I name the ones who I see a lot, the regulars, ya know?" he smiled. "Last year I was out by myself doing some maintenance on the platform, a large grizzly approached me, I had never seen him before, but he was enormous, the biggest bear I have ever seen. He was curious I could tell and so I remained calm, but then he got aggressive. He stood on his hind legs and was easily over ten feet tall, he growled and snarled at me. I pulled my gun out, but quickly realized that with a bear that size, my gun probably didn't have enough power to bring him down. I backed away from him, and he continued to pursue me. I thought for sure I would have to try to shoot him, I took aim when all the sudden a small cub ran right in front of the male. The baby distracted him and he came down off his haunches and chased after the cub. Suddenly, the mother bear, Sugar over there, chased the male down and attacked him, giving him a good swipe to the ear. I have never seen a male bear back down to a female bear like that, but suddenly the male ran off. Sugar showed that guy who was boss, and I think they must have known each other, because he knew she was serious about protecting her baby," he paused for a minute and looked at Ben and Lacey, "Hey guys what are you doing?"

Lacey was crouched next to the platform looking under it, suspiciously. Ben was pulling himself up a small tree that was next to the platform, searching everywhere for what could be the geocache. "Oh uh, they're looking for a geocache," Megan explained. "The waypoint leads to this platform, actually. Have you seen anything that could be a geocache?"

"A geocache huh? No, I can't say I have, that's like a small box of some sort, right?" he asked for clarification. Just as Megan was beginning her description, Lacey jumped in the air holding a small black metal box and hollered,

"FOUND IT!" as the words escaped her mouth she knew she had made a mistake, suddenly below Ben, in the thick bushes, a snarl tore through the air. The bushes rustled, and then separated. Ben was still in the tree, he climbed a little faster, Lacey stepped toward Trent and Megan, foolishly thinking that if they were on the platform the beast, which was emerging one huge paw at a time out of the brush, wouldn't bother them. She instantly realized she was wrong, she was absolutely wrong.

7

Ben's mom was getting a little anxious. She hadn't heard anything from Ben, Megan, or Lacey in two days. Knowing that they were most likely having a good time and just forgot, she saw no harm in logging onto United Cellular's website to begin tracking Ben's phone.

She tapped her fingers as the website processed the number and retrieved the proper information to place his location on the map. The site finally blinked with a red dot sitting next to Juneau, Alaska. What caught her eye and immediately sent shivers down her spine was the second dot she saw on the screen, this dot was marking all other cell phones that were linked to Ben's cell phone, and this dot was over a thousand miles away in the middle of Katmai National Park. She knew instantly that something had gone horribly wrong.

In less than a minute she had her phone in hand and dialed Ben's number, it rang, and rang and rang and just when she thought it would go to Ben's voice mail an older man answered.

"Yello," his voice was scratchy.

"Who is this?" Ben's mom asked.

"Who wants to know?" he snarled back.

"You have my son's phone, who are you?"

"Oh, my name is Henry, your son is Ben then, right?"

She felt a little relieved that Henry knew Ben's name, there must be some logical reason that he had Ben's phone, "Yes, Ben is my son, why do you have his phone?"

"Oh you know kids, he came to my diving shop to go explore a ship wreck and left his phone on the boat. Say, you don't know where I could find him, do you? I mean if he's still around town or something I could bring his phone to him." Henry smiled as a plot was developing in his head.

"Actually, it appears that he is somewhere in Katmai National Park. That's a long ways from you, why don't you just mail the phone to this address, do you have a pen?"

"Well, listen ma'am I'm sure there has to be an easier way, how did you know that he was in Katmai?"

"Oh, his phone, Lacey's and Megan's phones are linked through this United Cellular program, so I can find the location of the phones online," she answered. "Anyways, let me give you our mailing address, please just put the phone in the mail, that way it'll be here by the time that he gets back. I'm more than happy to pay for postage." Ben's mom proceeded to give Henry the mailing address.

Henry smiled as he hung up the phone, he moved his finger along the touch screen of the cell phone, until an icon popped up for "United Cellular Latitude" he pressed on the icon and suddenly a map popped up, he saw his current location, and then another red dot to the far left of the screen. They were certainly in Katmai, he decided. Now, how could he get to them? He decided to wait until their location changed, perhaps they would be coming closer to him and he could intercept them somehow.

"Hey, Henry, so um are we really gonna try to track the kid down? I mean they obviously were telling the truth, they're not looking for gold," Eddy asked.

"They aren't huh? How do you know?" Henry barked back.

"It's just obvious, I mean why would they be in Katmai now?"

"Here's another question for ya, why wouldn't they be heading home? Ben's mom just told me they were in Katmai, if you were his age and you had just been kidnapped, then somehow escaped, wouldn't you be headed home to your momma?" Henry sighed. "Nope, there has to be something big going on, something huge, to make those three continue on, they know something we don't and that is why they aren't heading home."

Henry paused thoughtfully and pulled on his beard, "I wonder now if Ben even threw the key in the air? Maybe he threw a pebble or something, he probably saved the key and just acted like he was throwing it to us. Yup, I bet that is exactly what he did, that little punk, sneaky. Plain old sneaky, which

just makes it clear to me; he is after something, I have no clue what it is, but it's gotta be good, and soon it's gonna be mine."

Eddy cleared his throat and glared at Henry, "Yours, how 'bout 'ours'?"

"Oh, yeah, I mean ours, *ours*. You're right, *ours*," Henry corrected himself, then stood up and walked to the coffee maker on the counter, "Over my dead body," he whispered to himself.

☙❧

Trent grabbed Lacey's arm and pulled her behind him. He kept his eye on the bear as he told Ben to stay put. He then pulled the handgun out of its holster, thinking for sure he would have to use it this time.

Ben looked down from his perch in the tree above the platform, everything seemed to be going in slow motion. Directly below him was an enormous bear, it had thick course brown fur that was long and shaggy, nothing like what he would have expected. He looked around and instantly became dizzy, *bad idea*, he thought to himself. He wasn't that high up, but every once in a while his fear of heights would rear its ugly head, now was one of those times.

"Ben stay in the tree," Trent commanded.

"No problem," Ben called back.

Trent continued to push Lacey and Megan back, until they had reached the railing of the platform and couldn't retreat any further. The bear continued to pursue them slowly, as it climbed onto the platform it stood on its back legs. It was easily ten feet tall, and it was angry. It growled fiercely as it swung its head from side to side, foaming slobber flew through the air.

Trent took aim, and then Ben interrupted him, "Uh… Trent you got company," he called down quietly. His voice was just enough to distract the angry bear standing below him, it turned and swiped at the tree, causing Ben to lose his grip, he slid down a few inches, screaming along the way. As soon as he got his grip, he climbed higher. The bear continued to paw at the tree, knocking branches and leaves to the ground. Megan cried as she watched Ben, helplessly.

Trent looked over the edge of the deck to see what Ben was talking about and noticed several bears coming out of the water, toward the deck, they were jogging and then suddenly began to run toward them. He wasn't sure what to do, he didn't even have enough bullets to hit each bear once, let alone kill any of the beasts. Something wasn't right. Even Sugar was running toward them, she had never displayed any violence toward a human. He again took aim at the large male that was attacking the tree that Ben was in, it had now begun climbing the tree.

"Good news and bad news guys! The bad: I'm gonna have to jump, the good: I don't have to go to the bathroom anymore!" Ben yelled, fear clinching his voice.

"Wait Ben, I'm gonna get this guy for you! Stay put," Trent pulled his gun back up and took aim, he had never had to use it before, and was clearly nervous. Just as he had his sights set on the bears head a sharp growl shook his entire body. Out of the corner of his eye he thought he saw Sugar rise up on her haunches, she took a step forward to Trent and growled again. Everyone froze.

"Uh guys," Trent said in a quiet voice, trying not to anger her anymore. "We have a problem."

"What?" Lacey asked.

"That's not Sugar," Trent informed them.

"What, how do you know?" Lacey asked.

"The eyes. Look this bear, it has blue eyes…I've never…seen this one before," Trent gently swung his arms over and pulled the gun up on the light colored bear standing before them, just as he started to press on the trigger the bear took a step forward and with its right paw swiped Trent's arm. The gun went flying over the edge of the deck and into the water. Trent backed up more, squishing Lacey and Megan as he clenched his bloody hand. "I don't know what to do!" he confessed.

Megan began to climb the railing, she would jump into the freezing water if she had to, she had decided. Just as she did, the blue eyed bear turned and lunged itself over to the tree, it grabbed the foot of the bear that was climbing up after Ben and pulled it down. Branches cracked and fell to the ground as the two bears attacked one another. Their snarls were so loud Ben could feel them shake his entire body. The two bears continued to fight, they were tearing into each other. Ben couldn't do anything to stop the horrific scene, he was terrified, but also so relieved the bear wasn't climbing up after him anymore. His only hope was that the light colored bear would win the fight.

Within a minute, the light blonde bear was pushing into the larger male bear's chest with her front paws. She had somehow gotten him onto the ground and was holding him down. Her fur was red with blood, no doubt her injuries were serious. Other bears were standing around the outer edges of the platform watching the fight, Trent was correct, this bear wasn't Sugar, as she and Cinnamon were amongst the onlookers watching this horrific event.

The blonde bear's mouth was wide open, she snarled showing all of her blood covered teeth, the brown beast under her wiggled and growled, but somehow was still pinned under her weight. She moved her mouth to his neck and bit hard, but not hard enough to tear through his flesh. She pulled up with a mouth full of fur, and again growled. This was her warning. The brown bear instantly understood and became calm. He was done either way, but he understood quickly that if he obeyed he would be walking away, if he continued to fight, he would not.

It seemed as though she was testing him, Ben thought. He stayed perched in his tree looking down on this amazing sight, checking back quickly with Megan and Lacey who were now both perched on the outer side of the platform railing. Trent was cradling his torn and bloodied hand.

The blonde bear slowly stepped off the brown bear's chest, and stood next to him on her back legs. She let one more fierce, terrifying growl cut through the air. Instantly, the brown bear rolled onto his legs and stood. It looked at Ben in the tree, and then turned sheepishly and ran away. The blonde bear looked at the rest of the bears, who were quickly making their way back to their fishing spots. She then turned and lifted her blood stained head toward Ben. She let out a weak snarl that was a combination of frustration and pain.

Ben stared at her for a moment, terrified this bear would now come up the tree, but she didn't, she just stood, staring at him. It was in that moment, when their eyes met that suddenly Ben knew, everything would be okay.

8

Ben steadied himself as he exited the plane. The wind had picked up, landing on the water had been quite an adventure in itself, not to mention the whole bear thing. He wondered, did he see things correctly? The bear's eyes had indeed been blue, they were the same blue eyes that had haunted and then saved him over and over again when they were geocaching in Oregon. Could the Keeper of the Lighthouse be here also? And if he was, how did he know where "here" was? Ben shook his head with confusion as he helped Megan off the sea plane and onto the rocking dock.

The water splashed the edges, drenching their feet as they slowly and steadily made their way to the shore. Lacey was holding onto the small geocaching container they had found at the platform, Trent steadied her so she wouldn't drop the container or fall off the dock. His arm was still bleeding, but the simple tourniquet he made out of his shirt seemed to do the job and quickly stopped the bleeding.

The group made their way to the cabin where they had originally checked in with Trent. As they opened the door, the thick heat enveloped them, it's warmth like a blanket, covered every inch, it was thick and dry, and instantly their gloves, jackets, and boots came off as they hovered over the hot wood stove.

"So how we gonna open this?" Lacey questioned.

"We could smash it? We could pry it open?" Ben replied.

"Why not just use the key?" Trent asked.

"An eagle took it." Megan said matter-of-factly. Trent just stared at her, she stared back, not willing to give more of an explanation.

"Okay..." he paused, "I believe you." Trent sighed as he shook his head. "Let me get a pry bar outta the shed, we'll get 'er open." He slipped his boots back on and headed out the door.

"So guys, not to put a damper on our fun or anything, but when do you guys wanna call it quits? I mean, this may never end, it may be one key after another after another, ya know." Lacey rubbed her temples as she spoke.

"I think we'll know when we're done." Ben replied.

"Yep, I'm with Ben, we'll let you know," Megan giggled. This was exactly the type of adventure she had been waiting for, she was so excited to find the next location, she could hardly contain herself when Trent opened the door to the cabin.

"Got it," He displayed the crow bar, as Lacey handed him the geocache. They put the small container on the floor and all stepped back as he used one foot to hold it steady and wiggled the bar under the lip of the container's lid. With one swift tug the lid popped open and a key bounced out.

"Yes!" Ben wailed, he bent down to investigate the key. It was the same as the others, small, brass, with a waypoint engraved on the back. He almost felt honored holding this. He was the first- only he and the "Cache Master" had touched the key before. Excitement shivered down his spine. "You guys ready?" he jumped up and down, like a boxer getting ready for a match, trying to calm the adrenaline that was surging through his veins.

"Yup." Megan said as she tied her boots.

Lacey was slipping her jacket back on talking with Trent. "Hey Aunt Lacey, you ready?" Ben yelled a little too loudly trying to break up their conversation.

"Yes." She snapped, then smiled at Trent again. "Wanna walk us out to the RV?" she asked.

"Sure!" Trent said, he grabbed his jacket, then slipped his boots back on. "So where's that key gonna take you guys?"

"Not sure, we'll check it on our phone once we get cell service." Ben replied.

"Well, if you end up needing a pilot, you know where to find me." He smiled at Lacey. They walked slowly down the steps of the porch from the cabin. Ben and Megan passed them, eager to get on the road. As Megan reached for the door handle of the dilapidated RV the entire vehicle shook. She gasped and jumped back.

"What the heck was that?" she shrieked.

"Guys, come back here, by us." Trent said calmly. They retreated and stood next to their aunt. Trent drew his gun, and slowly walked toward the RV which was now swaying back and forth and bobbing up and down. He peeked back at the rest of the group, and took a deep breath. As quietly as he could he grabbed the door handle, twisted the knob and then jumped back, gun still drawn.

"Come out with your hands up!" he hollered. Megan began to laugh, he peeked back to her. "What?" he asked.

"Nothing, nothing, it's just who says that? Ya know, 'come out with your hands up!'" she said in a deep male like voice. She giggled again and then Lacey slapped her shoulder for being rude.

Trent turned again and focused on the RV. It moved again, rattled, they could hear their belongings crashing to the floor inside. Ben prayed his laptop was okay. Suddenly though, his laptop wasn't his concern at all.

As they all stared mouths agape a huge black paw landed on the bottom step, it was followed by another, and then the massive body of a bear appeared as it slowly slid and sort of climbed down the stairs of the RV. The bear snarled and growled, but they couldn't see its face, and it couldn't see them, there was some sort of fabric on the bear's head.

Trent backed up to the group, his gun still drawn. "What is that?" he whispered. "A bandana?" he guessed. Lacey's face was bright red. The bear stumbled again pawing at the fabric blocking its view. Trent continued, "A towel? No oh look…there are leg holes…wait…are those butterflies? And wait…" He paused and looked at Lacey who was now bright red. "Are those…underpants?" he giggled.

Lacey desperately looked at Megan and then to Ben, and then a snarl broke their gaze. The bear had his head to the ground with one paw trying to grab the underpants off his head. They really were a perfect hat, almost like a shower cap, only through the leg holes poked the bear's large black ears. The backside of the underpants blocked his eyes and he continued to paw and growl as he attempted to get them off his head. Finally, one of his large claws got a grip on the waistband and pulled the underpants off, the sheer force sling-shotted them up into the air and they landed conveniently on a branch of the tree that was next to Trent. He paused and looked at the underpants hanging next to his head. Everyone stared at Trent, who then turned his attention back to the threat in front of him. Trent held his gun high and pulled the trigger once to sound off a warning shot to the bear. That quickly got the bear's attention and it ran sheepishly into the forest behind the RV.

Trent turned to see Ben, Megan, and Lacey lying on the ground, they had dove at the sound of gun fire, "Sorry, I should'a warned you guys that I was gonna shoot," Trent apologized, as he offered his hand to help pull them all up. As they stood, he looked to Lacey who was staring at her underpants hanging on the tree behind Trent. He turned and pulled them off the tree, then shyly handed them over to Lacey. Her face blushed even more; she quickly wadded them up, and shoved them in her coat pocket.

"Awkward," Megan announced, with an embarrassed look on her face.

Trent's face was just as red as Lacey's, he smiled then turned and headed toward the cabin. Lacey pushed Ben and Megan toward the RV, too embarrassed to speak.

"It's really okay, Aunt Lacey..." Ben said quietly, "I mean, at least they were clean."

9

"Well, that didn't take long." Trent said as Lacey, Megan and Ben walked back into the cabin.

"Yeah, we got out of the woods and had cell service, the next geocache, it's on Dutch Harbor." Ben replied.

"Dutch Harbor? Huh, really? Well then yeah you certainly need a plane then, don't ya?" Trent stood and grabbed his coat, "Let's go, we'll fuel up along the way."

❧❦

The sea plane bounced to a halt in the bay just off the docks of Dutch Harbor, Alaska. It was a tiny town, which was dwarfed even more by all of the fishing boats that surrounded the docks. There were huge boats, and small boats, nothing incredibly small, this was the Bearing Sea after all. Ben was semi familiar with the town, mainly from his obsession of watching crab fishing documentaries on the Discovery Channel. He got jittery and excited when he saw the familiar crab fishing boats that the show features, he so hoped to be able to meet some of the crab fishermen who he had grown to idolize season after season.

Trent gently parked the seaplane on a lower dock away from the large crabbing boats, the group unloaded and started a long assent up rusty metal stairs that connected the lower docks to the main docks above. The sea air had corroded the steel, nothing could last very long here. Ben knew from watching "Deadliest Catch" that a person could survive only a minute or two if they fell into the Bearing Sea. The ocean had a way of wearing down the earth's strongest materials, the salty air corroded and ate away at the steel steps, fresh wooden docks would weather and turn gray within weeks. This was a harsh area, Ben thought. This was an area that you didn't goof around in, it was too unforgiving. As they ascended the top step Ben nudged Lacey to hand him her phone.

"Okay, let's look at the waypoint again and see how far away we are." He started manipulating the phone's touch screen, "We have 53 degrees 54'18.41" North and 166 degrees 30'41.08" West." Ben paused waiting for the image to load on the screen. As soon as the image cleared up, Ben smiled broadly. "Ha, looks like this is gonna be an easy one," he said as he started walking across the large dock toward a large industrial building where the fisherman unloaded their catch by a huge crane.

The group walked alongside Ben, looking for anything that looked like a geocache. There really wasn't anything there, only a few sparse sea grasses lined the edge of the metal building. Besides random shells and an abundance of seagull droppings there was nothing.

"What do we do now?" Trent asked.

"Maybe it's not out here," Megan said as she eyed a large metal rollup door.

"Go inside?" Lacey questioned.

"Why not?" Megan responded. Lacey sighed deeply and rolled her eyes, this adventure was quickly becoming extremely stressful.

"I don't think we can all go in," Ben said quietly, "Why doesn't one of us just slip in and see what we can find?"

"Yeah right, Ben. I'm not letting you out of my sight again, weird things tend to happen to you at the ocean," Lacey shook her head with a look that said 'one hundred percent, out of the question.'

"Okay then, the two of us, let's have Trent and Megan wait out here, be a look out, we'll go inside, just for a second, and see what we can find," Ben waited for his aunt to shut down his idea, but was surprised when Lacey turned to Trent and asked,

"You mind staying out here with Megan?"

"Sure," Trent nodded, "No problem, as long as it's cool with Miss Megz?" he bumped her shoulder with his elbow.

"Whatever," Megan answered, she could actually use a bit of a break, she thought to herself.

Ben and Lacey broke off from the group and headed toward the side of the building, they didn't want to cause a scene by lifting the large metal door at the front of the building, facing all the fishing boats, and assumed there would be a smaller door, specifically for people to enter the building. As they headed up the side of the building, they saw what they were looking for, a simple, small, gray colored, metal door. They quickly slipped inside.

The air inside the building was heavy, it smelled of fish and sea water, not horrible, but certainly not good. They worked their way down a short hallway and came to a larger doorway. This door had a small glass window to look through before entering. Lacey lifted herself onto her tip toes to peer through the glass. On the other side of the window was a large warehouse space, lined with huge industrial size buckets that the fishermen would fill with either fish or crab. When full, these buckets would weigh easily a thousand pounds. The crane lifted the buckets to the dock where a large forklift would pick them up and drive them into this warehouse. It was in this space that the buckets would be sorted. Lacey counted six conveyor belts in the room, each belt disappeared behind a wall of hanging strips of plastic on the opposite side of the warehouse. Lacey assumed that workers would unload the large buckets, sorting the catch and then, place the catch on the conveyor belts which would then carry the catch to the other side of the warehouse. The thick plastic that cut the room in half on the other side reminded Lacey of a refrigeration unit. In places like this, where a constant conveyor system was moving into a colder or refrigerated area the plastic was thick enough to not allow too much cold air to escape, but also flexible enough to allow the catch to move the strips and allow it to come through and into that space.

"Let's avoid that side of the warehouse," Lacey nudged Ben.

"Okay, why?"

"There must be a refrigerated room or maybe even a freezer on that side, it could be dangerous," she responded. Ben nodded in agreement as he gripped the large handle on the thick door and slowly opened it.

They first went to the spot in the warehouse where the coordinates had directed them to on the outside of the building. They looked around the floor finding nothing. They separated for a moment, searching the walls and then finally looking up to the ceiling at the rafters. There didn't appear to be anything there. As they walked toward each other, Lacey's phone vibrated. She looked at the screen,

"Watch out," was typed, under a picture of Megan on her screen, the text message was a warning. Just as she looked at Ben, the large rollup door along the wall began to open. Lacey grabbed Ben's arm and pulled him to the wall, they quickly bent down and snuck behind some of the large buckets. Both held their breath as a large forklift began moving the buckets on the opposite side of the warehouse.

"What do we do?" Ben whispered.

"Let's just wait it out," Lacey responded. The two sat down and leaned up against the wall behind the bucket, peering around once every few seconds to see if they had a chance to escape. With his last peek around the bucket, Ben's heart jumped into his throat.

He grabbed Lacey's shoulder, "He's coming right for us!" he whispered loudly, as the bucket in front of them began to move. It started pushing backward as the forklift tried to wiggle its long metal lifting blades under it. Lacey was beginning to be squished against the wall, she panicked and pushed Ben, both narrowly escaped being squished. They ran from the side and hid in a small alcove space out of the view of the forklift driver.

The space was different than the rest of the warehouse, it hadn't been maintained at all and was filthy, loaded with large push brooms and industrial size mops. Just as Lacey was about to tell Ben they should bail out the large rollup door and just forget this whole thing she noticed something. In the farthest, darkest corner of the alcove, behind a roll of firefighter hose was a door handle. She motioned for Ben to look, they both went toward the handle.

"Should we check it out?" Ben asked. Lacey put her hand on the door knob, and tried to turn it. It wouldn't move, it was locked. She sighed in defeat and turned to see Ben holding up the key from the last geocache. He handed her the key, she rolled her eyes, there was no way this would fit, but the waypoint had pointed to the area, so she tried it anyway.

The key slid in slowly, she twisted it one way, nothing happened, it was still locked. Then, she twisted the other way and heard a click, she turned and looked at Ben, one eyebrow raised, mischievously. She slowly pushed the door open, the opening on the other side was dark and damp. The air felt different as it whooshed out of the room. Lacey and Ben stepped into the room and looked around. It was very small, the size of a small closet. They turned to one another, disappointed that they hadn't seen anything resembling the geocache in the space. Just as their eyes met they heard voices outside, it was one of the workers, they must have seen them as they hid in the alcove. Ben quickly grabbed the door handle and closed the door quietly. Just as the door clicked closed, the small room began to move.

"Are we in an elevator?" Lacey asked. She grabbed onto the doorknob, frantically trying to open it, but it wouldn't budge. The more she yanked on it the tighter it seemed to become. After a few seconds they felt a huge drop in the floor, and just as they regained their footing the floor seemed to fall more quickly. The force was so strong, they both grabbed onto the wall and looked down, they were free falling in the tiny elevator! The sound was deafening as steel scratched on steel. They looked around not knowing how to stop this thing, it just kept falling and falling, it reminded Ben of being on the drop zone ride in Las Vegas at the top of the Stratosphere Hotel, but instead of a feeling of exhilaration, fear was strangling him.

Suddenly, the small elevator crashed to the bottom of whatever space it had entered. It threw Ben and Lacey into the ceiling upon impact, knocking them both unconscious. The door to the elevator then opened into a deep dark space. In the darkness a figure emerged, it grabbed onto Ben's ankle and drug his unconscious body out of the elevator, leaving Lacey in a heap on the floor.

10

Ben's wrists burned, he slowly regained a throbbing consciousness. Opening one eye and assessing his situation he realized he was tied up, his wrists were cinched tightly, to the point of almost bleeding. His ankles were tied so tight his circulation was being cut off and couldn't feel his feet. The strange part was that he was hanging in the air, upon further investigation he realized he was entangled in a huge fishing net. Its thick rope was weathered and frayed, even though it was old it was at least two inches thick, he wasn't going anywhere. Even if he could untangle himself he soon realized he would be falling to a very uncomfortable end as he was being held about fifty feet above a very jagged and rocky bottom.

The room was dark, moist, and smelled of ocean—salty, moldy, fishy. Definitely not pleasant, he decided. He called out for help, but no one responded, it was eerily silent, except his labored breathing. Panic filled his chest and once again he hollered as loud as he could, "Anyone? Help, please help me, I'm stuck!" Again silence was the only response. He wriggled and swayed in the net, nothing seemed to be budging, he was certainly not here by accident. Looking up, Ben could see that this fishing net was being held by large rocks on the edge of a cliff, an underground cliff, he couldn't see the top of this vast space, there appeared to be no ceiling, only a thick darkness that seemed to be never-ending.

Ben began moving. The fight in him seemed to embrace flight and he was willing to do anything at this point to get out of the net, even if he fell to the rocks below. He hoped rather that he could free one hand and then somehow get enough control to climb the net up to the cliff above. He wiggled and twisted, the rope dug in deeper into his skin, burning and prompting him to stop. He paused every few moments to breathe through his pain and then somehow got angry enough to once again force himself to wiggle some more. As he wiggled one last time and somehow managed to free one hand he noticed something in the air, it was as if someone had opened a door or a window, a slight breeze maybe? Was it a sound, what sound was it? He thought and thought, he gripped the net as his hand was freed and looked down hoping to find an answer to his question. His eyes must be deceiving him, he thought, the rocks below were turning a bright orange color, slowly a wave of orange was creeping over the rocks, he focused more, determined to decipher what was happening. Then, suddenly he realized what the noise was. Below were thousands of crabs, a literal wave of enormous King Crabs, each at least a foot wide with two foot-long legs, creepy, crawling, climbing the rocks and the walls toward him.

    A shiver ran up his spine, he twisted to get a better grip on the net, he tore his skin as he yanked his other hand free, blood dripped from his wrist. As the blood dripped off his hand and fell to the rocks below the crabs piled on top of each other making a mountain, as they tried to get closer to their prey. Ben, still tied by his ankle, started climbing. The excess net under him hung in a large loop as he worked his way up. He shook his head to clear the hair from his eyes and suddenly the crabs below him were not his concern anymore, for above him lurked something much more sinister, something that Ben quickly decided was his worst nightmare.

ತಲ

A sharp pain pierced Lacey's rib, she slowly lifted her head as she carefully adjusted her body. A scratchy voice loomed above her and a heavy hand pushed on her shoulder.

"Hey, hey wake up, you okay?" The voice asked over and over. Lacey couldn't respond she was in between consciousness; she could hear but couldn't seem to force herself to respond. As the pain in her rib became stronger she was able to articulate nothing more than a whimper. Her brain was telling her to scream out; she needed to make sure Ben was okay, she needed to get back to Megan, she needed to figure out what was wrong with her and why she hurt so horribly bad. Her lists of needs were overcome by her reality, as she whimpered again she slowly opened her eyes, a shaggy blonde haired man knelt beside her.

The same scratchy voice echoed in her ears, "She's coming to, hey guys, she's waking up," followed by the sound and feel of heavy footsteps pounding the floor under her. Lacey gained enough energy, finally to speak, she began and found no air behind her words. She tried again, this time they came out more as a whistle than anything else.

"Ben, is Ben okay?" she softly whimpered in agony as the words crossed her lips. She looked up to the shaggy haired man, he had a friendly face, instantly she knew he was here to help and not harm her. His response didn't make sense though, she thought about his words and shook her head as firmly as she could as he repeated himself,

"Ben? Who's Ben? There's no one here but you." He looked up at the other men surrounding Lacey, all she could see were their large slimy rubber boots, she focused her eyes and looked beyond the boots, expecting to see the walls of the elevator, the industrial brooms, anything to verify her last memory. All she saw were blue buckets, large blue buckets, lining the walls of the warehouse she and Ben had ran out of. The only difference this time was that the buckets were filled with crabs, the conveyor belts were moving, slowly disappearing into the thick plastic sheets on the other side of the room, and humming five feet away from her was the large forklift. She looked it up and down, as if it would give her the answer to her question, and then as she focused on the thick, sharp metal forks a connection was made in her brain. She looked at the glossy red shine at the end of one of the forks, she followed the trail of red until she had to refocus and look more closely, she lifted her hand from the severe pain in her rib and just as she passed out she recognized that it too, was covered in blood.

II

The distant sound of a helicopter pulled Megan out of her daze, as it got closer worry began to fill her. It was coming right toward the docks and it was a coast guard helicopter which meant something was wrong, someone was hurt or missing. She nudged Trent, who had dozed off, and jumped to her feet, eager to see what was happening.

They both jogged over to where the helicopter was hovering over the ground, the sea grass swirled about and dust filled the air, as the helicopter landed a few men in orange coverall flight suits hopped out, they unhooked a metal and canvas stretcher from the side of the helicopter and started running toward the large rollup door in the warehouse that Ben and Lacey had gone into. Megan chased after them, but stopped outside the door as she watched them run into a crowd of men bent over someone on the ground. She looked more closely at the ground and gasped when she saw all the blood on the cement floor.

As the medics wheeled Lacey's unconscious body out, Megan and Trent chased after them, yelling and screaming questions out, "Is she okay?" Megan's voice broke as tears began rolling down her cheeks.

"Most likely a punctured lung, nope she's not okay." One medic responded.

"Where are you taking her?" Trent called out.

"Anchorage, are you with her?" the medic replied as he stepped onto the side of the helicopter.

"I am. I have to stay with the kids though. I'll call her sister, and we'll be there soon."

"Okay, and uh…" the medic paused not sure if he should finish his thought, "I'd hurry, if I were you."

The chopper began to lift off the ground, Megan and Trent guarded their eyes and ducked back toward the building. Megan sobbed as she dialed her mom's phone number. Trent grabbed her shoulder and told her he was going in to the warehouse to find Ben.

He ran into the building through the large rollup door, spotting the same group of men, he hollered, "Hey where's the kid?"

"What kid?" one of the men replied. "Aint no kid here."

"No, there was a kid with the girl, Ben. You didn't see a blonde kid with the girl that was hurt?" Trent demanded.

"Ben you say?" A blonde, shaggy haired man stepped out from the group. "The girl, she asked about a Ben too. This is a kid that was with her?"

"Yeah they came in here looking for a geocache, you didn't see 'em together?"

"All I know is I was loading up a bucket and my forklift hit something, I back up and she falls to the ground, bleeding like crazy. I had no idea she was back behind the bucket, but there was no one else, it was just her." The man wiped his eyes, clearly injuring Lacey had really upset him. "I'm really sorry man." He turned and walked back into the group of men, who all seemed to turn away from Trent to try to comfort their friend.

Trent went back outside, Megan said goodbye then hung up the phone.

"We've got a major problem," Trent said fearfully.

"What? Where's Ben?"

"That's the problem, no one here has seen him," Trent rubbed his forehead trying to figure out what had gone wrong, trying to figure out what to do. "Are your parents going to Anchorage?" he asked.

"They were booking a flight as I talked to them on the phone."

"Okay, well that's gonna take a few hours, we know that Lacey is in good hands, we gotta figure out where Ben is, as soon as we do, we'll be in the air.

❧❦

Horror filled every cell of Ben's body, he stared mouth wide open as he tried to think of something to do. The crabs were piling on top of each other below him, and above him a group of ghostly men were inching and edging their way over the edge of the cliff. They all stared down at Ben, eyes locked as they clung with the fingers and feet, almost spider-like to the cliff wall. Some used the rope on the net, others seemed to just float. The figures were translucent, the lines of their bodies were smudged, they flew and floated and all were speaking with deep scary voices.

"Ghosts?" Ben whispered to himself and shuttered as he closed his eyes and tried to get rid of the image. As he opened his eyes he let out a huge scream, directly in front of him was the face of a man, the translucent image was floating only inches away. Ben swung in the net, trying to free himself, anything to get away from the ghosts who were quickly surrounding him. They laughed at his effort, their ghostly, deep, voices echoing off the walls of the cavern they were in. It was too much, Ben choked on the fear in his throat, he thrashed and yelled trying to escape them, they danced and swayed inches from him, tormenting him with their yells, screams, and taunts. More and more of them came, each crawling and climbing down the cliff to where Ben was trapped, he continued to try to climb, although his efforts were sabotaged by the gang of spirits.

"Please!" Ben pleaded with them, "Please let me go, please leave me alone!"

Suddenly a ghost that was larger than the rest appeared inches from Ben's nose, "BOO!" he screamed in Ben's face, then laughed uncontrollably. The laughter was contagious and the entire group began violently laughing, the noise was unbearable. It boomed through the cavern, it rattled Ben's ears as if he were standing next to an amp at a concert.

The group composed themselves, then the large one raised his translucent hand and stretched it out toward Ben. Ben shrugged away from it, but soon couldn't escape and was forced to allow the ghost to place his hand on his shoulder. There was no weight to the hand, only cold, a cold pressure pushing down. Ben sighed trying to contain his unbelievable fear. "Who are you?" he stuttered.

"Captain Dwight." The ghost's face turned into a smile, he looked at his colleagues all floating and swirling around Ben.

"Are these your men?" Ben managed to stutter again.

"Oh no," Captain Dwight stated matter-of-factly. "We just hang out together, not a lot to do when you're dead." The captain laughed.

"Who…who killed you?" Ben stumbled over his words once again.

"Not who, but what…" the captain paused, "You're looking at the 'Bearing Sea's Bounty.' She took every one of us. One day we're fishing, the next we're dead. Some of us are from ship wrecks, others fell overboard, a few…" he leaned in closer to Ben, "Murdered." He whispered creepily.

"Wow…uh so what um…okay you gonna kill me or what?" Ben pleaded. Again howls of laughter filled the cave, ghosts started erratically flying, swooping, brushing up against Ben's back and face, they swirled around him, they shook the net which held him in the air, they shook in violent spasms and then disappeared, only to pop back up, out of thin air inches from Ben's face, he cried and hid his face. The laughter grew louder and louder, it hurt his ears. Then suddenly it was silent, Ben opened his eyes.

The captain leaned into Ben, he was inches from Ben's nose, he laughed one more time and then said, "Don't ya know…you're already dead!"

12

Henry and Eddy sat in the small cluttered office of the diving company. They hadn't mentioned Ben and the gold in a few hours, both were just waiting. Henry was waiting for there to be movement on Ben's phone indicating that the group was on the move again. Eddy was waiting for Henry to tell him what to do, both sat motionless until suddenly Henry hollered out,

"Okay, they are on the move, wow they be moving fast, too," he pointed to the dot on the screen of the phone, the dot that represented Lacey's phone, it was moving very quickly in the direction of Alaska's mainland. "Okay Eddy, we wait, that's all we can do, no sense wasting our energy until they obviously get to the gold or stop this silly wild goose chase."

Eddy nodded his head, he wasn't entirely sure that there even was gold, it seemed extremely unlikely that two kids with their aunt would even know about the gold on the Princess Sophia, but going along with what Henry wanted to do was much easier than questioning him, and so he played Solitaire on the office's old and slow computer as Henry stared at the screen of the cell phone he had stolen from Ben. Something would happen, he was sure of it, but he was pretty sure this entire chase was going to be a huge waste of time.

꘎꘎

The Coast Guard chopper landed carefully on top the Anchorage Hospital, a team was waiting and ran to the side of the chopper as Lacey was being unloaded, everyone yelled back commands and responses as to what she needed. They loaded her onto a hospital gurney and wheeled it into the entry way on the roof. Lacey could hear various things, she was in between consciousness and sleep, she felt as though she were floating, there was no pain, so it seemed silly that everyone around her was in such a panic. She wanted to cry out and ask where Ben and Megan were, but couldn't find the strength. Suddenly, she didn't have a choice as a bright light shone fiercely over her eyes, she couldn't move her arms to shield her eyes, she had to close them and then suddenly, there was nothing.

Ben was frozen, stunned he tried to speak and couldn't form the words. Captain Dwight giggled at Ben's shock, he then began laughing louder and suddenly there was a pressure on Ben's shoulder. He turned his head and was face to face with an upside down crazy haired ghost,

"Juuuuuust kidding," the ghost wailed in laughter, looked at Captain Dwight and said, "Did you see the look on his face?" Captain Dwight and the entire clan continued laughing, roaring with laughter until finally Ben yelled,

"Shut Up!" Everyone fell silent for a few seconds, they all looked around at each other, eyes wide and then once again broke into a huge thunderous laughter. Ben sagged his head. His feet were still tangled, his hands were free but if he let go now he would just be hanging upside down. Finally he decided to just calm down and play along with the ghosts. "Okay, okay guys…so what about helping me outta here?" Again there was silence.

"Well, that depends kid, what are you here for?" Captain Dwight asked.

"I'm just looking for a geocache, someone named the 'Cache Master' left it here for me."

"A what?"

"A geocache, it's just a game, you use longitude and latitude to find hidden packages, one of those packages is somewhere around here. I took the elevator down." Captain Dwight looked around at his peers, then moved closer to Ben,

"You say the Cache Master sent you?" he questioned.

"Uh…yup" Ben began getting nervous.

"Okay, okay, show me what he gave you?" Captain Dwight peered into Ben's eyes expectantly. Ben carefully let go of the net and reached deep into his jeans pocket, the cool brass of the key felt reassuring in his hand. He pulled the key from his pocket and held it in front of Captain Dwight's face. Captain Dwight's eyes lit up, his smile grew wide. He shushed all fishermen around him and then announced, "We've finally got it boys!" He reached up his hand and tried to snatch the key away from Ben, but as he grasped, his hand went right through Ben's, he tried again and each time no matter how still Ben stayed the Captain couldn't grab the key. Finally, other ghosts tried to retrieve the key from Ben, but no one could get their ghostly hands around the little brass key.

This gave Ben what he thought to be a wonderful idea, "Hey guys…guys," he said loudly to get their attention, "Why don't we work together."

Captain Dwight got a smirk on his face, shook his head eagerly and mischievously said, "deal."

As he said it, Ben suddenly got a sinking feeling in his stomach, something deep inside told him, he had just made a deal with the devil. His feeling didn't last long though, suddenly another feeling, that of being pulled up took over. The net he was hanging on was certainly moving, as it curved over the edge of the cliff Ben started to feel relieved, once his head was above the cliff however, fear instantly took over.

13

Trent and Megan searched the fishing warehouse for Ben, they found nothing, not a trace of him, it was as if he had never been there with Lacey. They proceeded out of the huge building and sat on the wooden docks that separated the building from the sea. Most of the fishing boats were out catching their bounty, and as far as the eye could see was nothing but water, thick gray water that connected to thick gray skies. Megan squinted, protecting her eyes from the overcast.

"He's gonna be okay, right?" Megan asked Trent.

"Yeah, don't worry honey, we'll find him, he may be hiding thinking they got in trouble or something."

"I hope you're right," she whispered back. "Do you think Aunt Lacey will be okay?"

"I hope so, I really hope so."

☙❧

In the darkness of the cavern a huge, enormous, car size king crab crouched. The creature's legs were easily twenty feet long, it's claws were something straight from a horror movie. The body was gigantic, the hard shell of the beast must have been a few feet thick. Its beady eyes moved around in circles and as they moved, water and air bubbles popped and hissed from they're bulbous sockets.

"You're kidding me, right?" Ben asked Captain Dwight who was now floating next to him. "What am I supposed to do with him?"

"He has your box, the one that key you got belongs to," Captain Dwight snickered. "And well please don't kill him, he's kinda the crown jewel around here, hundreds of years old, never once was caught in one of our crab nets, he's the true King of the ocean."

"I can't get the box from him, are you crazy?"

"Are you scared?" Captain Dwight laughed, "The Cache Master purposely put that box down here, knowing that whoever retrieved it really did deserve it. So, the question is, how bad you want it boy?"

"I'm not scared, I just, well look at him, it wouldn't be the smartest thing to aggravate something that could snap me in two," Ben waved his hand around nervously as he spoke.

"Your choice, but I'm pretty sure whatever is in that box, that's your way outta here." All of the ghosts surrounded Ben, they were mumbling and laughing. Eerie giggles filled the cavern and as they laughed their white outlines glowed brighter, illuminating the space. The added light allowed Ben to take a closer look at the beast before him, he saw a small box in the corner under the king crab, he just had to figure out how on earth he was going to get it. Suddenly, logic took over and somewhere deep inside a strength and courage rose in his chest. He felt confident he could take this beast on, and he refused to listen to the voice in his head that was currently screaming for him to stop.

Ben turned, knelt down, and took the large fishing net, that had previously held him captive, into his hands. With all of his strength, he lifted and tugged it over the edge of the cliff. As he looked down, the sea of red and orange crabs below him was continuing to grown deeper. Had he still been hanging in the net over the cliff they would have reached and consumed him by now.

He bunched the heavy net in his arms, and then laid it out in front of him, the ghost fisherman all moved to the side, as if their physical presence might actually interfere with Ben's placement of the net. He laid it flat, then stood in the center of the net.

Ben looked up to the ceiling of the cavern, on this side it was low enough that he could toss part of the net up and attempt to get it caught on the jagged rocks. The corner he chose had a long extra rope that would usually be used to pull the net up from the water. Ben took that rope in one hand and the heavy edge of the net in the other. He threw the net up toward the ceiling attempting to have it catch on the rocks, it fell with a thud to the ground. He picked it up a second time and tried again, nothing. With each throw the laughter from the ghosts got louder and the hissing sound from the crab became stronger. It lifted it legs, scratched at the floor and lifted its heavy claws which would fall with a commanding thud as they connected again to the rock floor. Finally, on what seemed to be Ben's twentieth throw, the net just barely caught the edge of the jagged rocks, it hung creating a curtain. There was still plenty lying flat on the ground for the plan to work, he thought.

Ben continued to hold the rope in one hand, then to the surprise of all the ghost fisherman Ben walked to the edge of the cliff where the jagged and sharp rocks protruded. He knelt down and with a shriek swiftly rubbed his forearm on the sharp rocks. As the rocks cut through his flesh, the wound started bleeding, it wasn't like the slow drip that his wrists had earlier, in fact they had almost scabbed over. No this was a thick stream of bright red blood. He carefully held his arm as he walked to the center of the net, and very silently shook his arm, staining the weathered rope red. Once he felt as if there was enough in the center, he walked out of the net and waited. Nothing happened for a few seconds so he pulled his shirt off and tied it around his arm. All of the ghosts were musing to themselves as to what this young boy was up to. After another minute, Ben's shirt began to slowly turn red from his bleeding arm, as the blood penetrated all the layers of the fabric Ben pulled it off and with his good arm threw the shirt as hard as he could at the enormous king crab in the corner. It took seconds for the crab to scoop up the small morsel in its claws. It pulled the blood soaked cloth to its mouth and quickly consumed the fabric. Once it had eaten the entire shirt it began to move faster, the blood had certainly ignited its senses. The crab's beady eyes bubbled and hissed, it moved closer to the net, its huge spider like legs working in unison to reach its goal. It stepped into the net, one claw at a time.

Ben held the rope tightly, he tried to conceal his bleeding arm, hoping it wouldn't distract the crab from the bait he had placed. Once the crab was halfway in, Ben couldn't wait any longer, he tugged as hard as he could on the net, it tore the slightest bit on the jagged rocks before giving way and falling on top of the crab. The crab was still distracted clawing at the blood on the net and ground. Ben used the opportunity to pull the net tighter, as he did the crab realized what was going on and began to fight him. Its large legs scrambled, it clawed at the thick rope, hissing and screaming through its eye sockets. Ben fought harder, trying to pull the net down and thereby forcing the crab to the ground but he wasn't strong enough. The beast was no match for the ten year old boy, its power was amazing, with each thrash of its claws Ben was being thrown and pulled by the rope- but he refused to let go. Finally, he realized that the crabs fight had only further entangled the beast. As quickly as he could, Ben began winding the excess rope around a large boulder that was at the edge of the cliff, after three loops around the boulder he got up and ran to the corner where the box was. He scooped it up and held it to his chest. As he turned, he saw that the crab was coming right for him, it was only slightly slowed by the net that was now tangled around most of its legs and the front half of its body. As fast as he could, Ben ran, he slipped past the crab then skidded to a halt right next to the large boulder. His toes were right over the edge of the cliff when he swung his arms out to catch his balance. When he realized he hadn't fallen relief crept over his face, he took one step back and turned just in time to see an enormous red king crab claw coming right for him.

The impact of the claw knocked the wind out of Ben, as Ben flew over the edge of the cliff he couldn't help but think that this must be the exact same feeling the baseball has every time he makes a homerun.

As his body connected to the sea of crabs on the floor of the cavern, he could feel their bodies breaking and snapping under his. He sank into the thick red claws and spindly scary legs, the sound of their hissing eyes surrounded him. Suddenly, his body began to scream in pain as they started attacking him. It felt as though a thousand claws were tearing into his flesh, he fought them off, kicking and hitting and swiping them away. Ben pulled himself to his feet, his balance uneven on their cracking bodies. He looked up quickly, begging for any sort of help, still kicking them away as they clawed their way up his pants. All of the ghost fishermen were floating above him, they couldn't help him so they just began screaming out commands trying to aid in any way possible.

Ben realized he was stuck. He couldn't run away from the torment of their claws, he cried out in agony as loud as he could, "HEEEEEEEEELLLLLLLLPPPP!" Suddenly, about ten feet away a figure appeared. Ben instantly recognized the long worn cloak, the staff he remembered pushing into his back when his journey had first began in Oregon. Deep within the cloak he saw the blue eyes of The Keeper.

The Keeper raised his staff and slammed it through the thick bodies of the king crabs until it met the floor. As it did, what appeared to be a shock wave started circling out from his cloak, the crabs lifted a foot or so in the air and then exploded into bright orange and gold dust. As the wave came to Ben, he too was lifted in the air and then just as quickly fell in a heap on the sandy floor. His body was bleeding and mangled from all the crabs that had tried to consume him. Ben looked up toward The Keeper as he floated toward him. The long twisted staff inched toward Ben's face, Ben grabbed the end of it and was pulled to his feet.

"Benjamin..." The Keeper whistled.

"It's you!" Ben sighed in relief, "You are the Cache Master!"

"No, no Benjamin. You finally called for help, and you finally accepted that you couldn't help yourself, and so as I promised, I am here." he leaned in closer to Ben, with his amazing height he had to bend over at the waist to get closer to Ben's face.

"I called for help before, in the net, why didn't you come then?" Ben was so exhausted he began to weep.

"Benjamin, do you know what happens to a moth if someone cuts it out of its chrysalis too soon?" Ben stared blankly at him, not understanding what he was trying to say.

"Uh, what? No, no, I uh, I don't get it," he sighed, defeated.

"When a caterpillar forms a chrysalis to change into a moth, it struggles for days building the strength to break free from the confines of the chrysalis. If someone comes along and cuts that moth out even one hour too early, the moth is not strong enough to survive on its own. It is only through our struggles that we gain strength, Benjamin."

"So in the net, I was building strength?" Ben questioned.

"Indeed, had you not scraped your wrists on the net, would you have known to lure the beast with your own blood?"

"But if you would have just come, then I wouldn't have had to fight the crab, I could have just gotten the geocache."

"Benjamin, I am not with you to aid you in your reward. I come when you are in your weakest moments, these are the moments in which you allow me to come. You see, sometimes admitting you are afraid...is the bravest thing you can do." The Keeper's body started to fade, it was almost pulsing.

Ben felt as though he needed to ask every question he could as fast as possible,"Okay, okay, how do I get out..." The Keeper began to disappear, "NO, don't go yet, please help me get out!"

The Keeper appeared once again, vibrantly, "First you must fulfill your debts, and then Benjamin, just..." his image started to flutter and flicker as it faded in front of Ben's eyes, "Swim." The word danced in the air, the whistling of The Keeper's voice was a music, soft, powerful, and every word meaningful.

"Swim?!" Ben yelled. The Keeper's eyes continued to glow as the rest of his body finally disappeared, and then just as quickly as he came, The Keeper was gone.

Ben looked around the cavern, a thick gold and orange dust carpeted the sand. He clenched the cold metal box to his chest. Strangely, he didn't feel any more pain, he looked at his arms, they were fine, his chest, also just fine, there was no evidence of any of the crabs biting him, clawing him, had it all been just a dream?

"So open the box!" Captain Dwight barked in his face. Ben had been oblivious to the ghosts around him. They had swarmed in as soon as The Keeper had vanished. Ben shook his head, trying to bring himself out of his state of confusion and fear. He lifted the metal box as he retrieved the key from his pants pocket. As he slid the key in the lock and twisted, the ghosts all began to whistle and scream, they danced and swayed in excitement, and then as they saw what was inside they got quiet and reserved.

"A key?" Captain Dwight asked. The other ghosts also questioned.

"Yeah, that's what's in every one," Ben responded. "Well, so far at least."

The younger crazy haired ghost that had been hanging upside down in the net next to Ben got in his face, "Yeah, it's the key, you guys, the key..." his voice got high pitched as he swayed and danced and flopped his hair around, "The key, the kid has the key!" he twisted and sang. Suddenly, they all began to rejoice, they whooped and hollered, they bounced and floated, their energy and outlines became vibrant, so vibrant that again they lit up the cavern. As they moved they parted into two sides creating a pathway, each was pointing toward the end of the pathway. Ben began walking toward the darkness, as he moved they moved, lighting the way. As he got closer, he could see a smooth rock surface, it was different from the rest of the rocks in the cavern, he placed his hand on the cold stone and slid it around. His fingers caught something, Ben looked closer, then looked at the ghosts.

"It's a lock." Ben announced.

"Well, DUH!" The crazy haired ghosts shot back, completely amazed at Ben's stupidity.

"You guys are locked in?" he asked Captain Dwight.

"Not anymore," Captain Dwight smirked.

"Wait, are you supposed to get out? Is there a reason you're in here? Did you do something bad?"

"We've done our time, boy, we helped you, you agreed to help us. Besides, this is your only way out too." Captain Dwight motioned for the door.

"Are you gonna hurt people if I let you out?" Ben stared at Captain Dwight.

"Did we hurt you?"

"Well, no...but..."

"Then you're gonna have to trust us." Captain Dwight peered at Ben more closely.

"Okay, you're…you're right." Ben mumbled.

"One other thing Ben, that key…it gets you out of here, and gets you into somewhere else. When you get there, remember us, the fishermen, just remember what we devoted our lives to, what we gave our lives for." The other ghosts began clapping and hollering.

"Right." Ben didn't know what Captain Dwight was talking about, but he knew at some point he would.

He lifted his hand toward the lock on the smooth stone, as he slipped the brass key in Captain Dwight yelled out one last thing, "Swim!"

Ben looked at Captain Dwight as the word echoed in the cavern, he was already twisting the key. As it made its final click in the lock a loud noise filled the room, and the door in front of Ben exploded into sand as a huge wave of sea water knocked Ben over and pulled him under. The salt water filled his mouth, nose, and throat. It burned his eyes, as he tried to right himself and gain control he noticed the water, it wasn't dark and clear, as it would usually be. This water was now filled with all of the dust from the thousands of crabs that had exploded under Ben's feet, this water it appeared, was filled with gold.

14

Ben kicked as hard as he could, the freezing water had numbed every inch of his body, except his lungs, which burned as they longed for oxygen. He looked at his hand for what had to be the tenth time, just to reassure himself that he hadn't dropped the key during all the chaos.

As soon as the seal had broken on the door, the ocean water had rushed into the cavern so violently, Ben didn't have a split second to react. He was overcome by the huge surge of water and had to use every bit of his energy to swim against the current and out the small doorway.

The pillars of the pier were a beacon of hope for Ben. As he pulled and kicked his way through the icy water, he passed them and then staying close by, pulled himself up in the water, one foot at a time, until finally he broke the surface. The chill of the cold air on his wet body instantly awoke the nerves throughout his skin as a surge of severe pain covered him. He looked up to the dock above him, it was far too high to pull himself from the water, but there had to be some sort of ladder or something, he thought. He moved down the length of the pier until he came to a rickety old grey ladder that hung from the top of the pier and disappeared somewhere beneath the surface. He grabbed ahold of the worn, weathered wood and attempted to pull himself up. He was so weak it took every ounce of strength to make it up one rung, he rested for a second and then pulled himself up to the next rung on the ladder, and the next, until he reached the top.

Once at the edge, he carefully pulled his body over the edge of the pier and sighed heavily, he opened his fist and eyed the brass key once again, "This better be worth it, Cache Master," he mumbled. As he spoke, he felt thunder beneath him, there was a pounding coming from the boards below, panic stricken he rolled over in an attempt to get up but couldn't muster the strength to pull his body to his feet. The thunder got louder and shook his body, he felt it in his chest, and head especially, pounding, pounding, pounding, and then it was broken with a shriek he recognized, followed by the screaming of his name.

"BEN!" Megan screamed at the top of her lungs. She was running at full speed to meet her brother who had just pulled himself over the edge of the pier about one hundred feet from where she and Trent had been sitting. The old wooden planks shifted and rattled as she and Trent ran to Ben's side. She was filled with relief, he was alive!

Megan knelt down next to Ben, his body was white, his lips on the verge of being completely blue, she pulled him into a sitting position and started hugging him as she rocked him back and forth.

"We've gotta get him warmed up." Trent said as he pulled Ben to his feet. "He has to move around, get his blood flowing, ya know." He was forcing Ben to move around, Ben was collapsing with each step, only to be caught by Trent, who was moving Ben's arms and dragging him around like a puppet.

"I'll go get help!" Megan began to run back to the fishing warehouse. A minute later, several men were running toward Ben with shiny silver blankets that appeared to be made out of tin foil. The men and Trent took Ben to the side, pulled off his wet, cold clothes and covered him with the blankets, then continued to force him to move around.

After a few minutes, Ben's color was coming back, the men brought him some dry clothes from inside the warehouse, he had gotten changed and was now eating his second Snickers Candy Bar.

Once he had a few minutes with the sugar in his system, it occurred to Ben that someone was missing, "Hey, where's Aunt Lacey?" Everyone froze, no one wanted to be the bearer of bad news, and finally Trent realized he had to say something.

"There was an accident, we're not sure how it happened, but Lacey is being flown to the hospital in Anchorage," he paused waiting for a response.

"We gotta get going then!" Ben yelled as he attempted to run in the direction of the sea plane they had flown in on. After about the fourth step his legs felt like jello and he collapsed onto the pier.

"Slow down buddy," one of the fishermen called out behind him. Once he reached Ben, he helped him to his feet. "Your body is in recovery mode right now, give your legs some time, right now the only thing your body can focus on is pumping blood to your arms and legs. Take it slow. By the way, where'd you come from?"

"Under the pier, there is a cavern, deep under water, it's guarded by a huge King Crab, big as a car, oh and a bunch of dead fisherman, I mean not *dead* fisherman, but ya know, their ghosts. I got the key from the crab, then I let all the ghosts out, the water pulled me out the door and under the pier, oh and get this! I saw The Keeper again! I know right? So random...anyways..." Ben continued going on and on about his adventure.

The men from the warehouse looked at Trent and Megan with extreme concern on their faces,

"He's way worse than we thought, you better get this kid to the hospital, he's delusional, clearly suffered some brain damage," the men looked at one another, shook their heads in sadness and slowly started walking toward the warehouse.

Ben shook his head and threw his arms in the air, "Well that was rude! Ask me a question and then just walk away, I hadn't even gotten to the part about the crabs turning to gold, whatever," he looked at Trent and Megan. "What?" Ben asked.

Megan looked up at Trent, "Maybe we *should* get him to the hospital."

Trent picked Ben up and threw him over his shoulder, then he and Megan ran toward the seaplane as fast as they could. Once everyone was buckled and ready to take off, they were airborne in a matter of minutes. Ben still didn't know what had happened to his Aunt, but he figured the silence could only mean one thing, whatever had happened it wasn't good.

As the plane flew over the rugged landscape, Megan looked closely at the coordinates engraved on the key she held in her hand.

She carefully entered the information into the GPS app on her cell phone, "Pebble Beach," she announced. "That's where this key goes."

Trent's eyes got wide, "Seriously? You sure?"

"I think so, the waypoint isn't right on the beach, but it's the closest named location, why?"

"Pebble Beach is the site of one of the most controversial future mine operations," Trent replied. "Scientists say that this mine holds the largest gold reserves in the entire world."

"Wow!" Megan sighed enthusiastically.

"Doesn't matter," Ben interrupted, "we're not going."

15

Megan hugged her mother as she entered Lacey's hospital room. Ben introduced Trent to his dad and then to his mom, who was already lecturing Lacey on safety. Lacey nodded and smiled as she tried not to close her eyes. She was exhausted, the sheer number of tests and scans and IV's wore her out. All she wanted to do was rest, and no one would leave her room long enough for her to fall asleep. She felt terribly rude, but couldn't keep her eyes open and dosed off mid-conversation with her sister.

Luckily, Lacey hadn't punctured a lung, the wound was superficial, so it only affected her skin and muscle, and while the gash in her side was large, it was easily fixed with stitches and staples.

"How did you guys get into this mess?" Ben and Megan's mom asked.

"We are doing a multi-cache, ya know? One geocache leads to the next, anyhow we just ended up in a warehouse and uh...well Aunt Lacey kinda got hit by a forklift." Ben explained.

"A forklift?"

"Yup." Megan interjected. She then looked to Trent for further explanation.

"Um, yes, uh Mrs. Conner...yeah, I have been flying them to some of the geocaches, it's really pretty cool. This was, of course, a freak accident." Trent did his best to try to convince Mrs. Conner that everything was okay. As he continued to explain things, Lacey woke up briefly.

"Hey, Ben, did you get the next key?" She was beginning to succumb to her pain medicine once again. Her eyes drooped as she spoke.

"Yeah, but we're not goin', not with you hurt."

"Where though?" Lacey asked again.

"It's a place called Pebble Beach." Ben looked at Trent, trying to tell him not to say anything about the potential gold mine. Lacey's eyes grew wide, suddenly she was fully awake.

"Pebble Beach? As in the Pebble Beach gold mine?" She almost yelled.

"Well, we don't know, it's just where the waypoint leads. You know how this goes, we don't know if it will be the last geocache or what, could be nothing." Ben responded.

"Or it could be everything, this might be the last one, Ben. Well hey, if you don't wanna go with me then I'll just take Meg, you wanna go, don't you?" She stared at Megan.

"Well, yeah, of course." Megan answered eagerly.

"Okay then, it's settled." Lacey relaxed a little bit.

"Forgetting something?" Mrs. Conner asked.

"Oh, yeah, thanks sis...Trent you mind flying us?"

"No!" Mrs. Conner interrupted, "Don't you think you should ask her mother?!"

"Oooooh, sorry sis, yeah, so is it okay?"

"Only if Ben goes too." Then she turned to Ben, "and your dad and I will stay here in Anchorage until you guys get back, then we can all head home."

"Yeah, okay," he replied. "What about the RV?"

"We'll figure that out when the time comes. For now go to this last geocache, see what you find and we'll decide if you want to continue after that." Mrs. Conner smiled at Megan, she knew how important this trip was to her, there was no way she would call it quits on her daughter.

Lacey dozed off again, this time everyone filed out the door and into the waiting room. Trent looked around the circle, "So I guess I'll be staying too, then."

"Do you mind?" Megan asked.

"Nope, not at all, but if there is gold waiting for you at Pebble Beach, I will have to increase my pilot fees," he joked. The whole group giggled, Ben and Megan went with their parents back to the hotel, Trent followed and got a room as well.

༄༅

Trent brushed his teeth and shaved with the complimentary hotel essentials kit in the hotel bathroom. As he walked back into the main hotel room his phone was vibrating on the night table indicating a new text message had just come through. He eagerly picked up the phone and read the text,

"what's the status?" The message read. He hit reply and wrote,

"convinced them 2 continu on 2 mine site, hopefully 2moro. I'll update then. Don't worry, u'll get ur $$$."

16

Lacey held her rib cage as the sea plane hit the water, she ached so badly, but also couldn't wait to see what was waiting for them at Pebble Beach. Once Trent slowed the plane to a slow glide, she released her firm grip, as she did the pain shot up to her shoulder. She secretly hoped this would be the end of their trip, it would all make sense, but somewhere deep down she knew, that this was potentially just the beginning.

"You okay back there?" Trent called out over the hum of the propellers.

"Yup" Lacey and Megan called out. Ben continued to read the article from national Geographic on Lacey's phone, she had located it for him in an effort to convince him that this was indeed a good idea.

The plane slowly pulled next to the dock, Trent once again got out and secured everything as Lacey, Megan, and Ben funneled out. One thing was for sure, United Cellular was going to potentially have a fit when they got the bill for Trent's services, Lacey thought, she couldn't imagine how much this was gonna cost when all was said and done.

"Well, let's get going on this, Aunt Lacey is gonna need to rest soon." Ben said as he herded everyone off the dock and onto the rocky beach. He eyed the slope in front of them, the hill wasn't steep and it wasn't huge, it wasn't really anything but a hill, Ben could hardly see how this was going to be an interesting geocache, except for the fact that it was located on approximately two hundred billion dollars' worth of gold and silver. The group started hiking a trail, following the GPS on Lacey's cell phone that indicated they needed to head inland. As they walked, the wind blew the wild flowers and coastal grasses that covered the landscape, they danced in the breeze, their simplicity was breathtaking, Ben thought. There truly wasn't a lot here. A few small shacks and cabins dotted the coastline, the hillside was very sparse, not a lot of trees or shrubbery, just a beautifully painted slope. It was what was in the distance on the top of the hill that had Ben concerned.

Ahead of the group on the trail was a tall cyclone fence, it stretched for what seemed to be a mile in both directions. As the group approached Ben could see a large "No trespassing" sign posted high on the fence.

Ben looked at Lacey's cell phone, "Well, we have a problem, looks like the geocache is on the other side of the fence, about one hundred and fifty feet past it, actually." he said solemnly.

"So, do we climb it?" Trent asked eagerly.

"Uh, I think I've learned my lesson about trespassing," Lacey said as she protected her bandaged side once again with her hand.

"We might not have to climb it," Megan called out, she was walking toward something along the fence line, "Ben, get over here and give me the key!"

Ben ran to her quickly, leaving Lacey and Trent staring at the phone. Once he caught up, he saw what Megan was headed for, it was a small entry gate, closed and secured with a thick metal chain and a pad lock. He wiggled the key out of his jeans pocket and started walking faster toward the gate. Once there he quickly put the key into the lock, turned it slowly, and it popped open. He was almost shocked at how easy that had been. Megan giggled with delight, there was no way she was letting this adventure end with a cyclone fence.

Ben called down to Lacey and Trent, they proceeded to head toward the gate as well, being mindful to close it and lock it behind them. Ben and Megan were already pacing out the one hundred and fifty feet to where the GPS had indicated that the geocache was located. As they walked and counted steps, both couldn't help but notice how barren this place was, besides the grasses and flowers there wasn't a lot here, it seemed as though there should be heavy equipment moving and making noise. There should be piles of dirt and tons of smoke filling the air; but on this day the blue sky was stunning, there was no sign of mining taking place at all. This felt more like a park than a mining site.

"One hundred forty-eight, one hundred forty-nine, one hundred fifty, okay, should be here somewhere," Megan announced. She stared at the ground as she and Ben walked in circles looking for anything that could be the geocache.

Trent and Lacey approached behind them and started looking as well, "The GPS says its accuracy is within five feet at this location, it can't be far," Lacey said.

"Yeah, if no one else has taken it already." Ben added.

"Who would know about it? You are the only one with the key, Ben, remember?" Lacey sighed as she continued to look through the thick grasses and flowers. Ben nodded and continued to look. This place almost felt wrong. It was too bare, there was nothing here.

He turned and looked at the horizon, "Wow!" he sighed. The expanse of the view was incredible. From this vantage point there was nothing but blue skies and sea. A few fishing boats floated on the crystal waters, besides that there was nothing. It looked almost like a painting, it was just perfect. Trent's voice interrupted Ben's stare,

"I think I got it!" Trent called out. He was on his knees, prying something out of the ground. Just as Ben and Megan approached him, the earth gave way around the metal box and Trent lifted it into the air. "Ben, the key, quick!" Trent yelled, his eagerness surprised Lacey, but even she was desperate to see what was in this box at such an important location.

Ben jogged over with the key and handed it to Trent. Trent inserted it and twisted, with a pop the box opened. He lifted the lid cautiously, then sighed when he saw what it contained.

"It's just another key," he groaned.

"What is the waypoint?" Lacey asked as she readied her phone to enter the information.

"It says, 62 degrees 26' 43.70" North and 157 degrees 58' 24.96" West." Trent sat back into the grass as he waited to hear where this key would take them. Lacey entered the waypoint into her GPS app on the phone and waited.

"We don't have to keep going," Ben said to Trent. "I know you want to, and thank you for all your help, but really we can stop. Aunt Lacey is hurting anyways, we should probably just call it quits."

"What would be the point though?" Trent closed his eyes. Ben was confused at Trent's reaction. He shouldn't be *this* upset about the geocache. Ben couldn't figure out what was going on with Trent, but he noticed that something wasn't right, Trent seemed stressed that the only thing in this geocache was another key. At this point, Ben wasn't even surprised by the outcome, he was more surprised that Trent seemed irritated at the situation.

Ben thought about it and then asked, "Ya know Trent, are you gonna be in trouble for being gone so long with the plane? Do you need to get back? Is that why you're upset?"

"Oh, uh...no this is fine, I just was hoping you guys would find what you we looking for, that's all." Trent reassured Ben.

Lacey interrupted their conversation, "Huh, is there really a town called 'Iditarod'?"

"Yeah, it's in the middle of nowhere, but yes there is, why?" Trent answered. "Gonna be snow there with how cold it's been this year though."

"Well, that's where we're headed." she looked at everyone, "That is if you guys want to go to the next one?"

Megan and Ben stared at each other, Ben knew Megan wanted to go, he wasn't so sure, but he would if his sister really wanted to, she had been talking about this trip all year after he and Lacey had won the prize the previous summer.

Megan looked at Lacey, "What do you wanna do, Aunt Lacey?"

"Hey you know me, I'll go anywhere," Lacey smiled, then looked to Trent, "Can you fly us there?"

"No, not with this plane, and not right now. I think there's only one way to get to it, actually most of the year there is only one way, well maybe two," he answered.

Lacey was confused, "Okay, how then?"

"Well I'm not totally sure but I'm pretty sure that you could probably only get their by snow mobile, or dog sled. You know the Iditarod Dog Sledding race; it's named after that town, obviously. One of the reasons is because of how remote the town is."

"So we get to dog sled?" Megan beamed with excitement.

"Or use snow mobiles," Trent answered.

Ben looked at everyone, "If the dog sledding race is named after this town, I only feel it would be right for us to use that mode of transportation. I think the Cache Master would want that."

Lacey nodded in agreement with her nephew, "Well said, Ben. Are you uh, coming with us Trent?" Lacey blushed as she asked.

"Uh, let me just text my boss and see what he wants me to do," Trent answered.

"If you're not using the plane, why would your boss care?" Lacey asked.

"Oh, uh...just um, you know to get time off work, that's all, I just need to ask." Trent pulled his phone out of his pocket, "You guys go ahead, I'll catch up."

Ben and Megan turned toward the fence, Lacey paused and looked at Trent as he typed his text message, then turned to catch up to the kids. Trent looked up making sure they weren't around, even though they couldn't see the screen of his phone, he was anxious.

"Nothing at the mine, but another key. What do you want me to do?" he hit send, then waited, he knew his boss was waiting at the other end and would reply as soon as he had received the message. Trent was so nervous he almost jumped when his phone vibrated.

The reply read, "Where r they goin' now?"

"Iditarod" Trent replied.

"Can't fly into there."

"I know, what should I do?" Trent typed.

"GET MY $$$!" the response made the hairs on Trent's neck stand up.

"I'm trying" he replied.

"Try harder boy, you're easy to replace."

Trent's jaw dropped, he knew his boss wasn't a patient man, but now he felt truly scared. As he slid his phone into his pocket, he glared into the distance toward Lacey, Ben, and Megan. The three of them thought this was all a game.

"They have no idea what's truly at stake," he mumbled to himself.

"You coming?" Ben yelled back to Trent.

"Yeah," Trent jogged up to the group.

"No, you comin' to the next geocache?" Ben clarified.

"Oh, yeah, my boss was fine with me taking a few days off."

"Great!" Lacey said, a little too eagerly, she caught herself, then to change the subject added, "You know, we need to get the information to United Cellular to pay you for flying us everywhere."

"Don't worry about that right now, we'll get that taken care of when I bring you guys back."

"Bring us back?" Lacey questioned.

Trent caught himself, he had almost said too much, "Oh yeah to your RV, remember it's parked at my cabin."

"Oh! Right, I had forgotten about that." Lacey smiled then turned and continued walking on the path, she had an uneasy feeling in her gut. She had seen a strange look on Trent's face. Was he hiding something? She wasn't sure, but suddenly she realized that they knew nothing about him. He was just a pilot, who worked out of a remote cabin. Then she remembered something that sent an instant jolt down her spine, when they had first flown with Trent, he had told them he worked alone, he said he owned the company. It occurred to Lacey that if Trent owned the company, he wouldn't have a boss. He was lying to them! She turned to confront him, but stopped herself as she noticed the handgun holstered to his hip. "Hey Trent, why do you have your gun?" she asked nervously.

Trent's eyes looked to his hip, then back up to Lacey, there was a bit of anger there, Lacey could see, "This is Alaska, Lacey, you never know what will happen."

"Oh , right, yeah sorry I'm just used to only seeing cops carry guns, ya know, in Oregon," she stumbled over her words.

"That's the other thing about Alaska…not a lot of cops up here," he stared into Lacey's eyes. "Lots of bad guys though."

17

"So where'd you get this plane?" Lacey asked Trent as he was gingerly landing it on an old abandoned airstrip in Ophir, Alaska.

"I borrowed it from a friend who owed me a favor, he's the one who told me about this airstrip too. It's as close as I could get you guys to Iditarod; you only have about ninety miles to travel from here."

"I hope this lady is for real, Ben found her on the internet, evidently she lives out here, raises her dogs and races every year in the Iditarod Race," Lacey held her rib as the plane touched down on the bumpy airstrip. She sighed in relief as soon as Trent brought it to a slow stop.

"Well, I'll wait here until you guys let me know if she's legit," Trent assured Lacey, "You okay? You've been acting weird ever since our last stop."

"I'm fine, uh…just hurting is all." Lacey looked away from him in an effort to hide her true feelings. She was hurting, but she was also terrified that Trent was somehow connected to Henry, there was just so much that wasn't adding up. She decided that she would play it cool for a while, not say anything until she could be sure that they were all safe.

&~&

The rocky tundra had sparse collections of snow around tufts of grass. What wasn't rock or snow was soggy and muddy from all the snow melt. Ben and Megan lead the way to a small hunting cabin along the tree line. The sound of the dogs helped verify they were in the right place, they could hear barking, growling, and howling. The yelps of the dogs surely were an indication of an excited sled dog team.

"This must be it," Ben called back to Lacey who was trailing behind.

"What's this lady's name?" Lacey asked.

"Sarah Hunter," Ben called back as he stepped onto the small porch of the cabin. Before he could lift his hand and knock, the door opened. Heat from the small space escaped and warmed his already chilled face. A young woman stood before him in the doorway, wrapped in a thick wool sweater.

"You must be Ben!" She beamed.

"I am, are you Sarah...err...uh...Ms. Hunter?" He quickly corrected himself.

"That's me, and call me Sarah. So you need to get to Iditarod, right?"

"Yeah, but how do we do that? There's not a lot of snow..." Ben sighed.

"Oh no worries, I have sleds with wheels. They won't even get stuck in the mud out here, so we're good to go. Why don't you come in for a bit, while I pack some rations." She motioned for them to enter her small dwelling.

Inside, there was an old, worn out loveseat and a wooden rocking chair, next to a small black wood stove. It was amazing how much heat was being emitted from the stove. Ben and Megan stood next to it, warming themselves, rotating their bodies every few seconds as the heat got too strong to tolerate. Sarah and Lacey went outside to a back porch area where they were packing food and chatting about life out in the wilderness.

"Hello," a soft voice called out to Ben and Megan, they turned quickly, startled by a young woman who had approached them silently.

"Hi, I'm Ben and this is my sister, Megan." Ben smiled at the woman.

"I'm Katie, Sarah's sister," she glanced nervously at the back door as she spoke.

"Oh, I didn't even realize anyone else lived here, will you be going with us today?" Ben asked.

"Yes, I think I should, I'll ride on the sled with you two, Sarah can ride with your aunt."

"How did you know she is our aunt?" Megan asked shyly.

Katie looked around nervously, "oh…um, thin walls, I can hear everything." Megan shook her head in understanding, she was just about to speak when she heard the back door creak open, as she looked back toward Katie she was gone.

"She must have had to get some stuff ready or something," Ben said, "Kinda weird though, I didn't even see her leave." He moved away from the stove and sat on the old loveseat just as Sarah and Lacey walked into the room.

"Okay, so we just have to get the dog teams ready, and then we'll be on our way, all the food will be on my sled. Lacey told me about her injury, and I think she better ride with me, I'll teach you guys how to run the team. Really the dogs know exactly what to do without being told," Sarah said as she pulled on an extra thick winter coat and hat.

"Yeah, it'll be fine, it's not like we'll be alone." Megan added.

"No of course not, like I said the dogs know exactly what to do, and you'll be following me so they'll know to stick right with my sled."

Megan and Ben looked at each other, both wondering why Sarah hadn't even mentioned Katie, but before they could ask Sarah was pushing them outside, loading their arms with supplies and directing them to two long dog sleds.

The sleds were about five feet long and two feet wide. The front of the sled sloped upwards the length of the base and created a triangle of fabric that connected to the handles. In the fabric covered triangle there was a lot of storage space, or extra space for passengers to ride in front of the musher, the person driving the team of dogs. That person, stood at the very back of the sled on a small platform, from this point they could help the dogs push the sled, going up a hill, or they could slow the sled down by using their foot or a brake lever that dug into the snow or ground to slow the team down. Sarah explained how the musher would lean from side to side as the dogs moved around corners on the trail, although the dogs know exactly what to do if something happens the musher gives the dogs directions, by a few simple words and whistles.

Sarah walked with Ben and Megan past a dozen dog houses, the dogs were yelping and jumping, they were so excited and seemed to be shouting, 'PICK ME, PICK ME!' As they were passed by, some yelped in sorrow, but then continued barking with enthusiasm. Sarah took one dog at a time and brought them back to the ropes and harnesses at the sleds. She explained how certain dogs are trained for certain positions on the team. Only a few dogs are capable of being the lead dogs out in front. These dogs cannot get distracted by anything along the path, and are in charge of the dogs following behind them. They set the pace for the entire group.

Sarah began attaching dogs to different areas along the lines, each dog was so excited to be going for a run. Sarah explained that

Waypoint Alaska

this is what these dogs live to do, this is the most exciting part of their day, when they get to do what they are trained for.

After organizing all the dogs and creating two sled teams Sarah went over the basic commands for the dogs, and how to maneuver the sled, she explained again that the dogs were mainly going to be following her team, so this should be just a simple ride for Ben and Megan.

Sarah had Lacey climb into the sled, she covered her with a blanket and then covered her with the fabric covering and attached it on the other side of the sled. She looked as though she had just been tucked into a very large leather boot, her legs were bent and she braced her feet against the boxes of supplies in front of her.

Sarah then moved over and directed Megan to climb into the interior part of the sled. As Megan slid in she made room for Ben, "Oh no sweetie, Ben is going to be driving the team from back here," Sarah explained. The dogs were yelping and howling, they were so eager to go that Sarah didn't even hear Megan ask about Katie. Sarah was obviously wanting to get moving. She showed Ben how to stand on the platform, made sure he had a good grip and then headed back to her sled. She pulled a metal stake out of the ground that was anchoring the team, motioned for Ben to do the same, then whooped a few times and the dogs took off. Ben's team started to move, following in line with Sarah's team, directly behind her sled. Ben looked at Megan, questioning what had happened to Katie, then suddenly he felt her jump onto the platform behind him.

"Sorry about that!" Katie apologized, she pushed Ben forward a bit, but didn't offer to stop so she could move into the interior portion of the sled with Megan. "This is okay, right? You want to learn how to drive the team, don't you?" She called into Ben's ear.

"Yes, uh…of course," Ben responded, not knowing how else to answer.

The sled's wheels rolled bumpily over the soggy surface as the dogs worked extra hard to work through the mud on the trail. Their team consisted of ten dogs. Katie explained how each was selected based on strength, personality, dominance and ability to handle stress. Ben was fascinated by their sheer strength and the fact that Katie hadn't said one word to them and they were moving together in a smooth effort to drag the sled. These dogs were incredible, he quickly decided.

As the team ran, Megan turned and began asking Katie a few questions. Mainly, what each dog was named, something flew beside her head and landed on the fabric next to her. She screeched and with her gloved hand brushed it off the sled, "Was that poo?" Megan dramatically asked Katie.

"Oh, yes, sorry. The dogs are so well trained, they don't even stop to go to the bathroom, it would take too much time if each of the ten dogs stopped at different moments to go, so they learn to literally, go on the run." Katie blushed a little, not knowing how Megan would take the information.

Megan smiled and looked at Ben, "Well that's something you don't see every day." She turned and settled in deeper into the sled, blocking her face.

"Will she be okay?" Katie asked Ben.

"Oh yeah, it's good for her, plus…well it's really funny for me to watch," they both laughed and then settled into the movement of the sled.

※

The dogs moved quickly, they maneuvered bends in the trail, around rocks and trees effortlessly, Ben and Katie didn't have to say anything to them the entire trip. As they came over a small hill, Ben saw a few tiny cabins in the distance.

"Oh what's that?" He asked Katie.

"That's Iditarod," she beamed.

"It's nothing though, is there a bigger part of the town up farther ahead or something?"

"Nope, that's it. There's only a few cabins left standing, it's a ghost town now, was abandoned decades ago after the gold rush."

"Gold rush?" Ben questioned.

"Yes, Iditarod was part of the first Alaskan gold rush, it was the lure for people from all over, they came, they mined, they built a small town. For a while it was a hub, and a lot of gold was extracted and sent away on the river. But as soon as the gold was gone, everything else was gone too. Life in the winter here is miserable, so everyone left. After years the buildings and cabins collapsed, so now there is just these ones left." She sighed heavily. "We usually don't see this place this much in one year, well only every other year when the race rolls through here as a check point."

"What do you mean?" Ben asked.

"Oh the Iditarod race, it has two routes, so on even numbered years, like 2010, it takes one route and then on odd number years, it takes another route. So on odd number years like this year, the race will go through the town of Iditarod. So today, will be my second time of seeing it this year. It's so the trail or the surrounding landscape doesn't get destroyed. Make sense?"

"Yeah, that's really smart." Ben acknowledged. "Sad about the town, though."

"That's what happens, people come for the wealth, and when that's gone, they leave."

Sarah's team stopped on the pathway right in front of the small cabin. There was more snow here, but still the earth was soggy, and the rocks were exposed in a lot of places. Ben's team of dogs slowed down and then halted right behind Sarah's sled, he laughed at how effortless this whole mushing thing was turning out to be.

Lacey climbed out of the sled and walked over to Ben, "That was fast!"

"Yeah, amazing isn't it." He motioned behind him to introduce Katie to Lacey, but realized she had slipped away, and was nowhere to be seen. He shook his head, wondering why she was so shy. Then realized Lacey was waiting for him to get the key out and see where exactly this geocache was.

He handed Lacey the key. Just as she finished entering the coordinates into her phone, it suddenly vibrated with a response, she smiled at Ben and Megan, "It's only ten feet away!" She turned and headed in the direction of a rickety cabin, "C'mon guys, it must be inside!"

Sarah followed the group as they entered the weathered cabin, she had seen it several times as she ran the Iditarod race but had never been inside. It was small, the floor boards creaked under their feet, slivers of sunlight shone through the wood planked walls. Ben and Megan began looking in the corners, Lacey looked above them at the beams of wood holding the roof in place. The black metal box, stood out amongst the aged wood, "Guys, over here," she called. Megan and Ben both came to her side.

"Megan, I'll boost you up." Ben bent his knees and put his hands together, creating a step for Megan's foot. She put her right foot in his hands, then they counted together to three. He lifted her easily, she reached and held onto the beam for balance with one hand, then grabbed the cold metal box with the other. Ben lowered her quickly to the floor.

Lacey took the brass key and slid it into the lock, everyone held their breath, thinking that maybe this would be the last cache of the Cache Master's game. She twisted the key slowly and the lock popped open. Even Sarah was enthralled with what could potentially be inside. Lacey lifted the lid and revealed another key. Unlike the other boxes, under this key was a slip of paper.

Lacey unfolded the paper and read aloud the words scrawled in black ink, "You've done well, I promise it will be worth your while." She looked at Ben and Megan, "Okay guys, decision time," she paused waiting for their response.

"Well, they are getting easier," Megan said.

"Yeah, that's for sure, and the note does say it will be worth our time, besides we really should be getting more pics for United Cellular," he reasoned.

"Okay, I'll call your parents when we're on the path back." The group left the cabin and loaded back up into their sleds.

"We should get a move on," Sarah said loudly as she pointed to the sky, "There's a storm coming in from the North."

Ben and Megan stared at the dark clouds blowing in quickly, "Yeah, let's hurry, we definitely don't wanna get stuck in that!" Ben called back to Sarah. With that, Sarah called out to the dogs and they barked and howled as they began pulling the sled again. Ben's team began moving once again, and just as before he felt Katie jump on at the last minute behind him. "Where'd you go?" he was almost annoyed at her rudeness, he still hadn't been able to introduce her to Lacey.

"Oh just wanted to check something out, sorry," she apologized.

"No worries, just seemed like Sarah was gonna leave you behind."

"She doesn't even realize…" she paused and then looked away, "It's okay, I made it, don't you worry I won't leave you guys behind." Ben glanced back at her as her voice chimed through the air, he did a double take when he noticed her beautiful eyes. They were an amazing shade of crystal blue.

18

The winds from the North were blowing stronger the further they got down the Iditarod trail, a mist was developing, hinting at the proceeding storm. The path remained bumpy, the wheels of the dog sled kept getting stuck in the thick soggy ground, even the dogs were acting a bit different, perhaps from the impending storm, Ben thought.

Sarah and Lacey's sled was about twenty feet in front of Ben and Megan's, the trail was winding through a thicket of tall pine trees. As Sarah's sled rounded a corner to the right, Ben's sled went left, he called out to the dogs, to halt, but none of them stopped. They pulled harder and more furiously.

"What do we do?" Megan cried out as she gripped the thick canvas sides of the sled.

"Katie, help! Stop the dogs, they got off the path!" Ben clutched the handle bars harder and continued to yell at the dogs.

"It's okay, they always head home." Katie reassured them, too calmly for Ben's taste.

"No, they are supposed to be following Sarah!" Ben yelled to her.

"Ben, calm down. I'm in control" Katie's voice remained calm, it was so soothing, and instantly helped Ben relax. "You need to learn to enjoy the ride, Benjamin."

"What did you just call me?" Ben asked, stunned.

"Oh sorry, Benjamin is your given name, correct?" Katie asked.

"Yes, of course, you just surprised me that's all," he looked at Megan, "Megz, we'll be okay. Don't worry." The bumps on the ground were shaking Megan like crazy, as the dogs continued to pull the sled faster and faster Megan realized that they were headed directly into the storm.

The landscape changed quickly, suddenly the wheels of the sled were becoming stuck in the thick snow underfoot. The dogs struggled, but somehow their leaps through the snow didn't slow the pace of the sled, if anything the snow helped it slide more easily for them. Ben began getting really nervous.

"What are we gonna do? Where are they going?" He asked Katie.

"They know where to go." Katie said reassuringly. Ben took a deep breath, then suddenly the sled stopped. Katie hopped off the back of the sled and took large heavy steps to the sides of the sled. She knelt down and quickly took the wheels off, they snapped off with ease, she handed them to Megan.

Megan looked at her, stunned, "Okay," she said, unamused. Just as quickly as Katie had gotten off the sled she was back on, Megan's head whipped forward as the dogs pulled the sled harder, now they were gaining speed easily. The storm was so strong and the falling snow so thick they could hardly see the dogs at the lead of the team. It was a pure white out. Ben shivered and closed his eyes, he wasn't sure what was happening or why.

The dogs continued to bark and pull as hard as they could, after an hour or so they came to a stop at something directly in front of them. At the sight of whatever it was, they all howled. It sounded as if they were crying with grief.

Megan turned toward Ben, ice had formed on her face where her eyes had watered in the strong freezing wind. "What do we do?"

Katie jumped off the sled into the thick snow and grabbed Ben's arm, "Megan, you too, come quick!" they both climbed into the deep snow, which was up to their thighs. As they struggled to the front of the dog team they saw a horrible sight ahead of them. Laying in the path was a large gray colored wolf, frozen blood covered the wolf's head and neck.

Megan let out a cry, "Oh my gosh!" She struggled through the snow as fast as she could to get to the wolf's side. Once she was next to it, she could see that the wolf was already dead. But something at the wolf's stomach was moving. Ben and Megan both knelt down with Katie as she lifted the stomach of the dead wolf, under her on the cold snow were three tiny wolf pups.

"Oh no!" Megan cried again, "What do we do with them?"

"If we leave them here, they'll die." Ben said solemnly.

Katie reached down and scooped the pups into her arms, "We have to put them in our coats, to keep them warm," she instructed Ben and Megan as she handed them each a pup. Both Ben and Megan unzipped their jackets and stuffed the tiny animals inside, where they nuzzled into their arms.

"Okay, let's get going!" Ben yelled to Katie through the thick stinging wind.

"There's no way we can get back now, the dogs are too cold and tired, we'll have to stay here tonight," Katie informed them.

"Wait, what?" Megan said, now agitated.

"C'mon, this storm is getting worse, we need to make a snow cave, it doesn't have to be huge, but we need it to fit all of us." Katie struggled through the snow and then about ten feet away from the sled started digging.

"She's serious?!" Megan cried to Ben.

"Yep, looks like it, we better help, or we'll freeze to death." They both joined Katie and as quickly as they could, scooped handful after handful of snow out of the same spot Katie was digging. After twenty minutes they had created a deep hole, and then had moved to the side of the hole, digging in and under the snow. They left about a foot of snow on top, to create a roof. Katie used her hand to smooth the top of the roof, smoothing it enough to make the snow melt just enough to form a stronger coating of ice.

The space under the snow was only five feet wide and maybe four feet deep, it was very small, but Katie assured them that this would be sufficient. Ben started climbing into the hole, when Katie interrupted him, "Benjamin, the dogs, help me, please." Ben looked at the dogs that were now curled into little balls, trying to stay warm. Most were almost totally covered in snow, except their snouts.

"Oh, they're coming in also?" Ben questioned.

"Of course! With this type of a storm, they'll die." Katie answered as she lifted a small bundle of fur and snow and walked back to the snow cave. She placed the dog in the entrance of the cave, then instructed Megan to go to the back of the cave to help situate the dogs as they brought them over. One by one Ben and Katie moved the dogs, and Megan tried her best to organize them in the small space. As the dogs cuddled down they formed a pile, all huddling together to stay warm. Ben brought the last sled dog over, then carefully squished into the cave with Megan and the dogs. Katie was retrieving something from the sled.

"Okay," she said as she carefully slid down into the hole. "You guys cuddle up with the dogs, I'll block the door here." Katie then tossed a small bag to Megan, "Those are the dogs treats, it's just moose jerky, so you and Ben can eat it too, but you'll wanna ration it." She leaned up against the wall of the snow cave and settled in. Megan noticed she didn't seem to be shivering at all, even though she was partly exposed to the outside storm.

"Aren't you cold, Katie?" Megan asked.

"I'm okay, not much bothers me." Katie smiled.

"It's actually not too bad in here," Ben said as he curled up closer to the dogs.

"Yeah, your body heat combined with the dogs will keep you guys warm enough, it won't be hot, but you'll survive," Katie wiggled a little bit then opened her jacket revealing the pup she had nestled inside. "Ben, can you hold this guy please, he needs to be a little warmer I think." Ben reached over took the pup and pushed him inside his jacket, the two puppies rubbed noses and pawed each other.

Megan unzipped her coat and scooped the puppy up in her hands, "Wow, look Ben, he's got blue eyes, so so cute!" Ben looked over, then he looked back to Katie, something told him this wasn't a coincidence.

※

Lacey paced back and forth in Sarah's small cabin, "We have to go look for them, they'll freeze to death!"

"We can't go now, the storm is too bad, if we go now and get lost then we'll all end up dead, the dogs know how to get home, they'll come back I promise, and your niece and nephew will be fine."

"So you're telling me you can't take me to find them, no matter what." Lacey scowled at Sarah.

"Pretty much, it's just too dangerous, I'm sorry Lacey."

Lacey flung herself onto the small loveseat, then pulled her phone out of her pocket and held it into the air trying to find a good cell signal. She stood up and wandered the cabin still looking for a signal, finally she went outside. The cabin door flung open in the wind. The freezing wind stung her eyes, but she continued to walk into the pelting snow. Finally, she had enough of a signal to make a call, she dialed quickly, not sure of how long she had before she would lose the signal again. The phone rang twice, then a familiar voice picked up, "Hey are you guys ready?" Trent asked. His voice was breaking up as the signal grew weak.

"No, we lost Ben and Megan, their dog sled went off the path up North, can you fly in this storm?"

"No way, I'm so sorry, but as soon as I can I'll let you know. If you hear anything from them, let me know too, have you tried tracking Megan's phone?" He asked.

"I haven't yet! Thank you, that's exactly what I'll do!" Lacey hung up and immediately dialed Megan's number. There was no answer, either Megan's phone had no service or wasn't turned on. She tried tracking the phone with the United Cellular Latitude mapping program, again there was no signal, a question mark was the only thing to appear next to Megan's name on the map. Lacey sighed heavily then marched back into the cabin. She sat on the loveseat again and started to cry.

"Tea?" Sarah asked as she pushed a streaming mug close to Lacey's face.

"Why not." Lacey said solemnly, she wrapped her cold hands around the mug and actually stopped crying, as she sipped the tea, she became more and more confident that Ben and Megan would make it, she prayed that somehow right now they were being taken care of.

After an hour of resting on the couch Lacey had fallen asleep. Sarah went outside to check on the dogs and give them warm water to help them stay warm. They were all curled up inside their dog houses, each came out, welcoming the warm water and the scratch on their ears that Sarah always treated them to.

After taking care of the dogs, Sarah walked over to a small space below a towering pine tree, she visited this space often. She knelt down and with a gloved hand scraped the snow off of three stone slabs, each had names etched into the white marble. "I wish you were here to help me right now, Dad." she said to one of the stones, her words disappeared into the wind. She paused, almost wishing for some sort of response, she knew she would never get one, but suddenly jumped as all the dogs rushed out of their dog houses and howled. Their howls cut through the wind, louder than she had ever heard before. She turned to see what they were howling at, there was nothing there, just the snow and the wind. The dogs returned to their dog houses, and Sarah turned away from the headstones. She walked back, over the frozen earth, to the cabin. She paused as she heard something in the distance. Through the wind, she recognized the sound of her other dogs, the lost dogs, howling. She couldn't be sure where they were, or how far, she knew at this point the only thing she could do, was wait.

⁕

Megan and Ben both jumped as the dogs in the cave all howled at the same time, in the small space the noise was almost unbearable. Just as quickly as they started, they all stopped and closed their eyes and returned to their deep sleep.

Megan looked at Ben, "that was random," she said.

"Beyond random, that was just weird." Ben settled back next to the dogs he was curled up with and closed his eyes. He was cold, but somehow not shivering, the dogs were creating a surprising amount of heat in the small, icy space. Just as he was dosing off to sleep, a small howl broke the silence and he opened his eyes. Ben looked at Megan trying to track the noise. There perched on her chest was the small wolf pup with the blue eyes. He howled again, a tiny baby howl, sounding like the cry of a human infant, rather than that of a fierce predator. Megan patted him on the head trying to shush him,

"No one can hear you, little guy, it's okay, settle down," she tried soothing him. The pup continued to howl for another minute and then turned around and returned to the warmth of Megan's coat. "So sad," Megan said, "He misses his mom."

"It'll be okay Megan," Katie interrupted, "Sometimes the tiniest voice, is the one that is the most commanding." Megan looked at Ben, confused.

Ben shrugged his shoulders and closed his eyes once again, then quietly whispered to Megan,

"Megz, get some sleep, you'll need your energy for tomorrow."

"Yeah, if we make it until tomorrow, this is just an epic fail!" Megan whispered back. She relaxed against the wall of the snow cave, wrapped her arms tighter around the pup in her coat and closed her eyes. Sleep came easily, as did more and more snow. Neither Ben nor Megan knew that by morning—they would be buried alive.

19

As Ben opened his eyes, a crystal blue light seemed to seep through the snow and into the cave. He looked around, eyeing all the cave's inhabitants. There was Megan, resting next to several sled dogs, with the small wolf pup tucked under her neck. The ten sled dogs were all cuddled up in a heap trying to remain warm, and then Katie, who was resting next to what was the door. This morning there was no door and only snow. Ben began to panic, had it snowed that much the night before that they were now snowed in? How would they get out? Was there enough oxygen in this small space with all of these inhabitants to maintain life?

He began hyperventilating, "Katie, Katie, wake up!" He nudged her with his foot.

Her eyes opened and she looked around, "Shoot, it did snow a lot didn't it!" she said loudly which in turn woke Megan and all the sled dogs up. "We better start digging, it looks like it may be sunny out there." Katie started pushing on the snow that had covered the entryway to the cave. Ben handed the two pups that were in his coat to Megan and then began helping Katie dig. They continued to push snow, but found themselves getting stuck, it seemed that the original hole they had dug to build the snow cave was now full of snow, so their entry point was no longer available. "Ben, we've got to get out of here, lay on the floor and start kicking at the ceiling," Katie commanded him.

"But, but...won't all the snow cave in on us?" He questioned.

"Yes, but there will be a better chance of surviving that than running out of breathable air," she responded. Ben did as he was told. Megan squished up against the furthest wall with all the dogs. Ben got into position and then as hard as he could began kicking the ceiling of the cave. The surface was icy, from the condensation of their breathing all night long. As he kicked, little pieces of ice broke off and fell on his face, finally he was through the initial ice layer and hitting actual snow. As he kicked more and more, larger amounts of snow were breaking loose and falling into the cave. Finally, he had broken through and created a hole to the surface. From the inside of the cave it looked as though about three or four feet of new snow had fallen in the storm.

Ben continued to kick around the small hole. More and more snow fell and then suddenly, there was a cracking sound, right after the sound the entire roof of the cave came crashing down. Everyone was crushed to the floor. The dogs all began yelping and squirming, their whines and whimpers were the only sign of life.

☙❧

Sarah and Lacey were busy harnessing up all of the dogs to their dog sled. They knew they must hurry, their plan was to ride the trail then exit where Ben and Megan's sled team had. Lacey was receiving a good signal from Megan's phone, she hoped that finding them wouldn't be too incredibly difficult. They attached all of the dogs, grabbed some extra water and food, and hopped onto the sled. Sarah called out to her team and they took off, running through the thick fresh snow.

Lacey was impressed with how smooth this ride was compared to the one the day prior. With the wheels on the sled the ride was bumpy, and although the dogs could easily haul them even through the soggy earth, today they moved much more freely. The weight seemed to be lifted from the team, they moved in unison and the sled easily slid over the surface. She prayed once again that

Ben and Megan would be okay, with everything they had been through, this couldn't be where their story ended, could it?

◈

Ben was roused by the movement of all the dogs. He felt snow being tossed around, large pieces hitting his body and then he felt the pain in his chest, he tried to breathe and only got a mouth and nose full of icy snow, he tried moving his arms, they were pinned under the snow's weight, he was trapped. As the thought occurred to him, he began to panic even more and suddenly he realized that if he was trapped, then so was Megan. Suddenly, he got a wave of adrenaline and began kicking and moving, even the slightest bit was giving him even more space to maneuver. He moved and pushed more and more snow away, his lungs burned, his head felt dizzy and painful, he knew soon the lack of oxygen would be too much, if he wasn't fast enough he would surely pass out. Using all of his strength, he took his fist and punched upward as hard as he could. He could feel his hand exit the snow, fresh air wasn't that far away! He moved his hand around more and more and then took his other hand and punched through the surface with it. Then he wiggled his legs under his body and used his last bit of strength to push the top half of his body up.

As his head and face broke through the snow, he could feel the icy shards slicing his lips and cheeks, he brushed the snow from his eyes and inhaled deeply. He looked around and saw the mess of the cave-in. Out of the corner of his eye, he saw a small bump in the landscape where the dog sled had been. It had snowed so much the dog sled was completely covered and would take ages to dig out.

He wrestled with the snow more and more and moved over to where he thought Megan should be, he began digging as fast as he could, throwing large chunks of ice and snow over his shoulder.

Finally he found a tail. He grabbed onto the dog's tail and yanked as hard as he could, he heard a muffled yelp and then saw the snow move more and more as he pulled the dog up and out of the collapsed cave. Once he had one dog out, others used that exit point and began clawing and fighting to get out as well. The hole became bigger and deeper and Ben continued to dig, using the dog's movement and disruption in the snow pack to aid in his rescue effort.

By the time Ben's hand hit a hard rubber surface, it felt as if too much time had passed. His tears froze on his face as he dug around the grey colored snow boot. He pulled more and more snow out of the way, calling out Megan's name with less and less sound behind his wails due to his lack of energy. Finally, he had followed her leg up to her waist, he continued digging. Once he uncovered a gloved hand, he grabbed on as hard as he could and began pulling, the snow was so heavy he couldn't get enough weight to force Megan's body out.

He yelled at the dogs who were now prancing and eating clumps of snow, "DIG!" When he yelled this he really didn't think they would understand or do as he requested, it was a moment of desperation, but every single dog ran over and next to Ben began digging. Their paws cut through the snow much faster, their strength was unmatchable. Second by second, as snow was being throw behind each dog more and more of Megan was being uncovered. Once there was only about a foot of snow covering the top half of her body, Ben once again, using all his power pulled on her arm. The snow above her broke free and slowly fell off, as her body slid out from under it.

Her skin was blue, her face torn from the snow. Ben removed his glove and carefully placed two fingers to her neck, trying to see if she had a pulse. She did not. Ben froze, he didn't know what to do, suddenly all of his training in first aid was forgotten. He grabbed onto her face and yelled at her, he lifted her blood stained head to his chest and rocked back and forth.

As he did this all of the dogs came over and began licking her face, some jumped onto her body to get closer. "Get back!" he yelled at them, thinking they were only licking the blood from her wounds. But with each lick color was coming to her face, Ben saw what was happening and felt under her neck once again there he felt the softest of thumps. Her heart was beating. Ben moved her around more and more, he knew he had to get the blood moving faster through her body.

He sat her up and tried to move her arms and legs and then all of the sudden a sound escaped Megan's lips, "Kaaaatiiieee," she whistled softly. Ben got closer to her face,

"What? What Megan?"

"Katie, don't leave me," she said softly and slowly.

Ben looked around, he had totally forgotten about Katie. He motioned to the dogs and said,

"Help me find Katie!" Ben and the dogs ran over to where he was motioning. The dogs sat and looked at each other, not knowing what to do. Ben saw their hesitation and yelled again, "DIG!" the dogs quickly began to dig, and they got deeper and deeper in the snow, but found nothing. Ben got down on his knees in the deep hole they had created, right where the entrance to the cave had been and continued lifting chunks of snow away, there was no one there.

Ben yelled at the dogs once again asking, "Where is she?" There was of course, no response. He was exhausted and scared. He went back to Megan to make sure she was okay, she had started to come to and was rubbing her bloodied face. He sat next to her, weeping, not knowing what to do about Katie. He sat for a few minutes, sure that Katie was dead. The pups in Megan's jackets were all wiggling and whimpering, licking her neck and face. Megan was smiling, relief filled Ben's face.

"BEN! MEGAN!" a familiar voice screamed out in the distance. Ben helped Megan stand as they turned toward the voice. Approaching from the South were Sarah and Lacey, being pulled by their dog team. The loose dogs ran over to greet their friends, their tails wagging so fiercely their entire bodies shook. Lacey practically fell out of the sled as she was trying to get out quickly enough to get to her niece and nephew. She ran to them, still holding her side and struggling through the thick, deep snow. She pulled both of them into a big hug, tears of joy streaming down her face. "Thank God!" Lacey wailed.

"How did you find us?" Ben asked as he welled up with tears also.

"The GPS on Megan's phone, this morning as soon as the storm passed we got a signal, we came as fast as we could. Thank God you're okay!" She pulled them in tighter.

Sarah approached from the side, "I knew you guys would be okay!" She also pulled Ben and Megan in for a hug.

"Sarah, I uh...I have bad news." Ben paused, confused as to why Sarah wasn't already questioning where Katie was.

"The sled? It'll be fine Ben, we'll get you guys back, don't worry." Sarah patted him on the shoulder.

"No, we...we can't find Katie, she was in the snow cave with us, then it caved in, I was able to find Megan and get the dogs out but we have searched and dug and we can't find her! I'm so so sorry, I don't know what to do." Tears were streaming down Ben's face now, he had never been in a situation like this before.

He wiped his tears and looked at Sarah, her mouth was agape, her eyes wide, "Ben what did you say?"

"We can't find Katie, she was with us, ya know sledding and everything, and now…now she's gone."

"Katie? Katie who?" Sarah was almost becoming angry.

"Katie, your sister…she looks just like you." Megan interjected. Sarah shook her head and turned around, she paced for a second, clearly upset.

"I…I can show you where she was sitting, I can help you dig more, but it's been a long time, she's…I mean she's been down there a long time." Ben's head dropped in total defeat.

"I just…I just don't know what you're talking about!" Sarah yelled, "Are you trying to be funny? Are you seriously making a joke, or something?"

"What? No, no, not at all, why would we be?" Ben cried.

"Ben, my sister, my twin sister, Katie…" she walked closer to Ben, Megan, and Lacey, looked at them with terror in her eyes, "Katie died when we were born."

20

The howls of the dogs sent a chill up Ben's spine. The air was still crisp and cold, but the snow was slowly melting in the sun's bright light. The days ran into nights here, as it was summer and Alaska was getting about twenty hours of daylight. Ben wasn't sure if the lack of sleep was messing with his mind; or if he was simply imagining things, but as he stood over three grave stones he knew something very strange was going on.

Megan interrupted his silent thoughts, "So this is it, this is Katie's grave?"

"Yes, my mother died while giving birth to us, shortly after, Katie died as well. My father raised me out here, and two years ago he died. I've been alone ever since." Sarah answered. She dusted the loose melting snow off of Katie's tomb stone.

"This grave so small, but have care, for a world of hopes are buried here." Ben read the tomb stone's engraved words aloud, *"Katie Hunter, March 5, 1980."* He shook his head and looked toward Megan, "I wasn't just dreaming all this was I, she was real wasn't she? You saw her right?"

"Yes," Megan answered quietly and shivered. She felt grateful for Katie's help, but also strange that they had been conversing and spending the last two days with a dead person.

Ben turned to Sarah, "She looks just like you, the only difference is she has crystal blue eyes." Lacey quickly turned her head and stared at Ben, "I know, right?!" He proclaimed at how strange this all was. Sarah dropped her head, and sighed as she wiped another tear from her eye.

"That's just hard for me to believe, I've...I've been alone for so long, with only the dogs out here..."

"Well it's true, I know it sounds like we're making it up, but really Katie was with us, she built the snow cave, she pulled the dogs in, she took care of us. I think she was the reason the dogs went off course, if they hadn't we never would have found the wolf pups. You're not alone out here, Sarah." Ben fell silent to let his words have impact. Sarah starting crying heavily then turned and walked away.

"Speaking of wolf pups," Megan interrupted, "Do you think mom and dad would let me keep one?"

"What?" Ben paused, "You know what, they just might actually, which one do you wanna keep?"

"'Compass.'" Megan announced. She opened the top of her coat and a small black nose poked out, "I named him, fitting don't you think?"

"I think it's perfect." Lacey said as she rubbed her finger along Compass' muzzle, "Wow! Look at his eyes!" Lacey said excitedly. She looked at Ben expectantly again.

Ben nodded his head, "This is what I'm talking about, so strange, right?!"

"Absolutely!" Lacey agreed, "We better call Trent, make sure he's ready to fly us down South."

"South?" Megan asked, as she zipped Compass back up into her coat.

"Oh yeah I forgot to tell you guys, the next geocache is on a glacier! It's called 'Mendenhall Glacier' I talked with Trent he's gonna have skis put on the plane for landing on the ice, wicked huh?"

Megan looked at Lacey, "No. I mean yes, that's very cool, but you, well sorry Aunt Lacey, but *you* can't pull off a word like 'wicked' you need to stick with 'cool' or 'neat,' just sayin'." she giggled to herself then looked at Ben, *"It's crazy wicked!"* she teased Lacey.

"*Really?*" Lacey rolled her eyes at Megan, then thought twice, "Okay, you're right." She relinquished. "Anyways' it's really neat though, right? Skis on a plane!"

"Very neat." Megan agreed.

Ben motioned for them to follow him up to the porch of Sarah's cabin, he tapped gently on the door. "Come in." Sarah called out from inside. Ben opened the door and stepped into the small warm space.

"We're gonna get going, is it okay with you if Megan keeps this one wolf pup?" he asked.

"Of course, just remember Megan that a wolf pup isn't going to be as easy to train as a domestic dog, so be careful. I'll take care of the other two, they'll make great team dogs, I think."

"Thank you." Megan replied.

As the group stepped back out onto the porch, the entire group of sled dogs cried and howled. Ben looked over at them and saw Katie standing at the edge of one of the dog houses, she had her arms up, calming the dogs down, then turned to Ben and waved. Sarah stepped next to Ben and looked in the direction he was looking,

"It's so strange when they do that, they'll be so crazy noisy and then all the sudden they are silent and all looking a certain direction." She paused for a second in thought, then with a questioning look, turned to Ben, "Is she...I mean is Katie doing that?" She shivered and the hairs on the back of her neck stood up.

"She is." Ben answered, not sure if Sarah was ready to believe him.

Sarah shook her head then replied, "Amazing."

Ben, Megan, and Lacey walked in the direction of the landing strip, in the distance they could see Trent standing outside the plane, waving excitedly. Ben and Megan looked back toward the small cabin and there they saw Sarah and Katie standing next to each other waving at them. They both waved in return, Ben yelled out, "Bye Sarah, bye Katie!" They both called goodbye back. Ben watched Sarah turn directly toward Katie, she paused for a second, almost as if she could see her, then continued toward the cabin. Just as Sarah stepped away, Katie disappeared.

Ben turned back around and caught up with Megan and Lacey. Trent was just starting the propellers on the small plane, their sound blocked out all other noise as it dominated the air. They all climbed on the plane and got buckled in. Megan immediately loosened her coat to allow Compass to stick his small head out and sniff around. As the plane took off, the only sounds that could be heard were the loud humming of the engines and the soft howls of the orphaned pup.

His cries brought a lump to Ben's throat, "Thank you, Katie. For helping us find the wolf and her pups," Ben whispered to himself.

"No worries." Katie said back. Ben jumped and quickly looked to the seat next to him, Katie sat next to him smiling, then just as quickly as she had appeared, she was gone.

21

The bright glare of the ice was almost blinding. Megan quickly pulled her sunglasses down over her eyes. Her boots crunched on the thick ice beneath her feet. The spikes on her boots stuck an inch into the surface to prevent her from sliding. Every step was work, every step was incredible.

The group was walking on over one hundred feet of ice. This was once water that had flowed down and froze to form this glacier, perhaps millions of years before, carving out mountains and canyons in its path.

"Trent, you think the plane will be safe?" Lacey called back to him.

"Oh yeah, there's no one else out here but us, we shouldn't be long, anyways. Isn't this geocache just up here another two hundred feet or so?" Megan suddenly knocked on the side of Trent's head. "Ow!" Trent hollered, "What was that for?"

"Knock on wood, never, ever, never say 'we shouldn't be long, this is an easy one.'"

"You knocked on my head though!" He complained.

"Uh, *yeah*…do you *see* any wood around here, it's the next best thing." She giggled then said, "Seriously though, you're gonna jinx us."

Lacey looked back to them, "C'mon guys, I'd like to get done with this before dark…" she caught herself realizing it barely ever got dark here during this time of year, "I mean dinner, before dinner."

Ben laughed then announced, "Guys another hundred feet and we should see something." He walked faster, his boots crunched into the ice, ahead of the group. He continued in the direction Lacey's cell phone indicated they should go. As the group hiked more, they followed a small pathway that seemed to be cut down into the glacier's ice, after approximately seventy five feet the pathway dead ended and was surrounded by walls of ice over twenty feet high.

"What should we do now?" Megan asked. They all stared at the walls of ice that towered above their heads. Streaks of blue and gray interrupted the white ice, as if someone had taken a paint brush and painted strips of color randomly on the white frozen canvas.

Ben peered up and noticed a small disturbance in the ice at the top of one of the ice walls.

"I think we have to climb up to get it." He pointed to where he was looking, there on top the ice was the corner of a small black box. "How do we get up there?" Ben asked Trent.

Trent sighed and whipped out a large ice ax, "You use two of these for your hands, and the spikes on your boots to get a grip for your feet." He turned to the opposite wall and drove one ax in the thick ice. It cut into it and stuck in place. Trent then wiggled it out of the ice by pulling up on it and handed it to Ben.

"Uh…" Ben looked at Megan, she sighed in annoyance and then grabbed the ax from his hand.

Megan took a step toward the icy wall which held the black box and slammed the ax above her head into the ice, she then raised her right foot and as if taking a forceful step up slammed it into the ice, she lifted herself up and took the other ax and cut it into the ice above the last ax, then followed with her left foot. She worked her way up, crunching and cutting the ice as she climbed.

Trent, Lacey, and Ben looked up in awe of this little girl. She was small, but she was a powerhouse of strength, and had not one bit of fear when it came to heights.

As she came to the top of the wall, she peered over the edge, the ice on the other side was rugged and cracked. She now understood why they had to climb to this geocache rather than just hiking to it. Hiking on that unstable ice would have been crazy dangerous. Megan pulled herself over the edge and stayed laying on her tummy as she dug the black box from the ice. She used one of the ice axes to break the ice and snow away from the sides of the small box, then eagerly slid it from its frozen safety.

"Got it!" she called down. She looked over the edge then tossed the box down to Ben who was holding his hands out. Megan pivoted her legs over the side of the wall and quickly found her footing with her ice boots, once again creating her own steps as she kicked the spikes deep into the ice. As she lowered herself something in the distance caught her eye, there was movement to the left, at the beginning of the trail leading to where they were. She listened harder and squinted her eyes. Her mouth dropped. There in the distance were two men that she recognized, crunching through the ice on the same trail they had come in on, Henry and Eddy.

Megan turned her head and quietly called down to the group below her, "You guys, Henry and Eddy, they're on the path, they'll be here soon!" Lacey and Ben's eyes grew wide in fear.

"Megan, jump down!" Ben called up to her.

"What? No! There's no way out that way, you guys climb up!" she called back frantically. They all three looked at one another, "I'm gonna toss my axes down, watch out!" Megan yelled in a whisper. Trent stepped to the side, scrunched up with Lacey and Ben as Megan dropped her axes. He handed them to Ben who sighed deeply, closed his eyes, then moved quickly to the wall.

He followed Megan's method and worked his way up, his forehead dripped with sweat, not from the exertion but from the fear building inside of him. Megan helped pull him up and over, then once again they tossed the ice axes down into the small area below.

"You, go ahead." Trent motioned for Lacey, she accepted his offer without thinking twice and slammed the axes into the ice, quickly stepping and pulling herself up the wall. Finally, she threw the axes down to Trent, who was looking down the pathway, just as he heard the axes fall he also heard the crunch of footsteps in the distance.

Trent grabbed the axes and dug them into the wall, climbing up just as he had shown the group, he was just as fast as Megan, and barely frazzled at all. The group looked at each other and then looked at the ice field that spanned out before them. Jagged crevasses filled the landscape. The ice was weaker here, the top layer unstable.

"We have no choice," Trent interrupted everyone's thoughts. He grabbed Lacey's hand, "Everyone hold hands, if one of us falls we'll be like a safety rope."

They each took a step forward, some of the ice broke beneath their feet, creating instant anxiety. Trent lead the way, they followed the jagged, narrow wedges of ice at the surface. They stepped gently and methodically. Trent explained that if the ice broke they could fall into a crevasse, which was a huge crack in the ice. Sometimes these crevasses went hundreds of feet deep, into the glacier below. Once in them, there was little or no way out.

Trent continued his methodical planning with each step he lead the group on, they were only thirty feet from the wall they climbed up when they heard a man's voice in the distance.

"Well, looky here!" Henry yelled to them. Eddy's head appeared next to Henry's foot as he climbed over the edge of the wall and joined his friend. Lacey looked at Trent, who didn't seem surprised.

"How'd they find us?" She asked. She glared at Trent and let go of his hand. He stared at her, not knowing what to say or how to answer her question. "How'd they find us, Trent?" She yelled at him, slowly pushing her niece and nephew back away from him.

"What? I don't know?" Trent replied as he shook his head.

"You told them, didn't you? You work with them, right?" She yelled at him.

Henry's voice interrupted her, "Now, now Lacey, don't be upset, you don't wanna yell out here, you'll crack the ice!" He took a step toward Lacey, Ben, and Megan, balancing himself on the narrow patches of stable ice. Lacey pushed Ben and Megan further away.

"Lacey, I don't know what you're talking about!" Trent called to her. Lacey was pushing the kids harder now, making them move faster away from both Trent and Henry, who were both advancing in her direction. Eddy started to follow Henry as he eyed Trent.

Lacey began panicking, looking back and forth as Henry and Trent moved faster and faster toward them, "We trusted you!" Lacey yelled between sobs, just as she yelled a loud cracking noise rumbled below them, and suddenly the ice was moving. First Megan fell, Ben followed, and right as Lacey began to scream she started her free-fall into the crevasse that had opened up beneath them. It swallowed them whole.

Lacey landed on top of Megan in a heap on a cold icy floor. Around them, chunks of thick ice poured down, she instinctively covered her head. Looking around through the shower of ice she saw Ben laying on the ice next to them, he too was covering his head, Megan was moving under her, she knew they were both alive and for the most part, okay.

The shower of ice stopped and silence filled the space. It was long and narrow, dark and scary. Ben looked up and could see only a small sliver of light above them, he wiggled over to Lacey and Megan and whispered, "Are you guys okay?" They both nodded, afraid to speak for fear of the ice breaking below them and falling into another crevasse. "We can't climb back up. We'll have to wait for Henry, and Eddy, or Trent to throw us a rope or something." Ben tucked his feet under his rear-end as he crouched next to his sister and Aunt.

"Was Trent really working with Henry?" Megan asked quietly.

"I think so," Lacey answered, "How else would they have found us?" Ben thought for a second,

"I never would have thought he would be a bad guy." They all fell silent as they realized the danger they were in. "But the good news is, they'll have to get us out." Ben lifted his hand out of his jacket pocket revealing the small black metal box, "If they want this, that is."

Megan stood carefully and tested her legs, after the fall she was achy and in terrible pain, she wanted to insure nothing was broken, as she stood she noticed another fragment of light coming from the far end of the crevasse, "Hey guys, check it out, this might be another opening." She motioned for them to follow her.

Carefully, Lacey and Ben stood, they each stayed to the side of the crevasse and crept along, moving slowly. The walls of ice got closer together, and above them all light disappeared as they advanced down the narrow cave-like structure. They continued to walk in the darkness, Lacey pulled out her cell phone and pressed the screen button, it illuminated the space just enough for them to feel safe walking in the darkness.

After only another twenty feet in the narrow passage way of the crevasse, the group squeezed through a small opening and entered a large open space. The walls were thick ice of the glacier, above them light shown through a thick icy ceiling. Hanging from the icy ceiling were large icicles, each at least six inches wide and some over four feet long. The space was vast, the layers of ancient ice were a variety of colors ranging from deep grays to reds and then crystal blues. The silence was incredible, only a random drip from the icicles broke the stillness of the space every now and then.

"This is incredible," Ben announced quietly. "These icicles could kill you if they fell, when they get this big they should be called the death cicles." He paused thoughtfully, "Looks like our way out isn't really a way out though," he concluded solemnly as he looked above them at the thick ice ceiling.

Lacey looked back at the direction that they had entered from, "I think I hear something…" she held her hands up motioning for Ben to be quiet. They all listened, in the distance they could hear arguing and yelling. They heard Trent holler out in pain, then they heard Henry and Eddy yelp and next a thunderous echo entered their space, a sound they realized was that of the men either falling or jumping into the crevasse where they had fallen in. Ben grabbed his sister's and aunt's hands and pulled them to the furthest wall of the cave. They stood, knowing they were in plain sight, but hoping that somehow it would give them more time to react.

"What are we gonna do?" Megan whispered, trembling. A light shone down the narrow passage way they had just come from, it bounced and gleamed off the icy walls, it danced along the long icicles that hung from the ceiling. Ben looked around anxiously, he held Lacey's arm tighter. Trent, Henry, and Eddy squeezed through the opening and stood at the opposite side of the cave. Megan asked again, "What are we gonna do?"

"I have no idea." Lacey whispered back, her voice shook, "I have absolutely no idea."

22

"Just gonna leave your little boyfriend behind, were ya?" Henry teased Lacey as she cried. He was busy tying Trent, Lacey, Ben, and Megan together with a ragged piece of rope.

"He's not my boyfriend, besides it's clear he's working for you anyways," Lacey snarled at Henry.

"Working for me? Huh well that would have been a good idea, but no, I don't know your boyfriend here." Henry explained as he finished and stepped away from his masterpiece. "Now, I would like to thank Ben here for putting such a lovely tracking device on this here cell phone." Henry showed Lacey how he'd been following their every move using the United Cellular Latitude app on Ben's phone. When he'd had his fun he returned to Eddy who was carrying the group's ice axes back to the opening in the crevasse so he and Henry could climb out.

"You weren't working for him?" Lacey asked Trent over her shoulder.

"No, of course not, I don't know these jerks!"

"Why did you lie to me then? First you said you owned the tour company and the plane was yours, then later you said you had to ask your boss about taking us to Iditarod." Lacey waited patiently for a response.

"I…I said I owned the company 'cause I was trying to impress you. The truth is I do have a boss, it's a small company, so I run things at that location, but no, I don't own the company. I…I just thought that you would think I was some back country hick or something, giving tours, I mean you're in college and you have a future." Trent dropped his head in embarrassment.

"Uh, I don't mean to interrupt this little confessional, but Trent do you still have your gun?" Ben interrupted.

"I do, I can't get to it though, it's in the back of my pants, in the waist band." Ben shifted his weight and leaned in toward Trent, their hands were all tied together, it was a stupid move really to tie them all together but Henry only had one piece of rope, and frankly didn't appear to be that smart, Ben rationalized. Ben felt the handle of the gun by Trent's back, he tried to grip it with his fingers, but had no luck, his gloves were too thick, there was no way he could get a good enough hold to pull the gun out safely.

"I can't get it with my gloves on," Ben announced.

"Get what?" Henry barked at the group. Ben's back was to Henry he had no clue he'd returned to the cave. Henry marched over to the group and kicked Trent in the leg. "You hiding something?" He growled. Then in a fit of rage, he pushed Trent down so his face was almost touching the ice, revealing the hand gun in the back of Trent's pants. He grabbed the gun quickly and pointed it at Trent. "Well looky here, didn't think a kid like you'd be packin' heat."

Megan couldn't contain herself, she was beyond terrified, and also just really sick of Henry. She was sick and tired of being bullied and well—just over it, suddenly she burst out laughing, "'Packin' heat' *REALLY* Henry," she laughed harder and looked at Ben. Then in a mocking gangster style voice said, "*Hey bro, this gangstas gonna put a cap in us.*" She laughed even harder, "I mean seriously OMG Ben we are going to be killed by complete morons!" Suddenly she was angry, she glared at Henry then said, "If you're gonna do it, just do it, it's cold down here and I'd rather die from a bullet than freeze to death!" Her voice echoed through the ice cave. Lacey and Ben both looked over their shoulders, amazed at the words coming out of her mouth.

Henry had had enough of this little girl's tantrum, he raised the gun above his head, clearly not thinking about where he was and pulled the trigger. The explosion of noise made the group freeze, then suddenly it wasn't the noise that was the problem, the ceiling of the cave began cracking and falling down in large chunks of ice, the huge icicles released and slammed into the floor exploding into millions of glass like shards that sprayed the entire room, the group lowered their heads in an effort to protect themselves, then suddenly the entire roof collapsed, crushing Henry and a bewildered Eddy, who had come running toward the cave as soon as the shot sounded.

Just as the last of the large ice chunks shattered to the ground the floor of the cave began cracking. The noise was terrifying, it sounded as though a huge earthquake and volcanic explosions were happening all at once, the ground shook, and a large crack started over by where Henry and Eddy's lifeless bodies were laying covered in ice. The crack spread quickly, over to where the group was sitting on the floor. It then circled the group, Lacey screamed as she watched, almost in slow motion. Suddenly the ground opened up, and all four were falling, still sitting on a large chunk of ice. It felt like ages, as they free-fell through layers and layers of ice, which shattered under their weight. Finally there was one last explosion, Lacey looked up and saw the entire cave collapse, above them, then as the chunk of ice they were sitting on hit water, all four bounced off and slid into its freezing depths.

They were all fighting to get air, the cold water stung and stabbed at every inch of their exposed flesh. The current of the river was strong, as they fought each other and the motion of the water, the rope untied and their hands were free. One after the other, their heads popped up and they all gasped for air. Surrounding them were other large chunks of ice. The river was flowing under the glacier, the water was crystal clear, and freezing cold. Trent grabbed onto the side of a large chunk of ice and pulled himself on it. Then he reached out for Lacey, and hauled her up over the edge of his makeshift raft. Once he had her out of the water, he grabbed the hood of Megan's coat and yanked her up over the side. Ben was floating further away, as he saw what Trent was doing he swam to the nearest piece of ice that was large enough to hold him and lifted himself onto it.

"What the heck is this?" Ben called out to the others.

"It's called a 'mulan' it's a river that flows under a glacier!" Trent answered.

"Okay, where does it go?" Lacey shivered as she asked.

"Sometimes they go underground, but they always lead to another body of water." Trent assured her. He put his arm around her and pulled her close, "It's gonna be okay, at least we don't have to worry about those guys anymore," he said reassuringly.

Megan relaxed a little then said, "I'm so sorry you guys."

"What? Why are you apologizing, you just saved us." Lacey put her hand on Megan's shoulder.

"If I wouldn't have gone off on him though, he wouldn't have shot and we'd just be figuring out how to climb out of the cave right now, not floating down a mulan or whatever this is."

"True," Trent said, "But he could have just shot us."

"I guess," Megan mumbled. "We don't even have the key anymore though, this whole thing was pointless."

"First of all," Ben answered back as he used his hand as paddles and brought his ice raft closer to the side of the ice raft Megan was sitting on. "This wasn't pointless, second of all, good call Megz on forcing us to buy this water-proof 'under armor,'" he said as he pulled on the collar of his undershirt, "and third," he put the fingertips of his glove in his mouth and pulled it off, as the glove came off a small bronze key dropped onto the ice he was floating on, "We still got the key."

He smiled at his sister, who's eyes were wide, "How did you? When did you?" She questioned eagerly.

"When were standing against the wall waiting for them to come into the cave, I knew they were gonna steal the black box, so I took the key out and relocked the box." Ben smirked, "Just like you said Megz, they were morons."

"Yeah," Megan smiled, "I guess you can't fix stupid." She relaxed a bit and leaned up against Lacey's leg.

As they continued to float down the river, the passageway the water had carved would grow small and then large again, the ice that towered above them was incredible, in some places they could touch the ceiling, in others all they could see was darkness above them, as the vast caverns seemed to go on forever. The layers of the ice were incredible, they passed huge boulders that were encased and frozen enormous trees. They could only guess as to how old each was.

The water moved slowly enough that Ben could paddle around and pull himself to the icy walls of the glacier. He was bored with the slow movement of the water and so began pushing himself toward one side of the river, only to spin on his ice raft, and then push off against the opposite wall, causing him to zigzag across and down the water. He was floating in front of Lacey, Megan, and Trent, who were relaxing and resting their eyes, as if they were floating on some sort of inflatable float at a resort somewhere, completely safe.

As Ben bounced back and forth across the river, he saw a strange movement in the water along the right wall of the river ahead of him. He paddled closer to it, indulging his curiosity. As he approached he saw that the water was swirling, it was a slow movement, so he didn't really think anything of it, he pulled his raft closer. With his final pull towards the swirling water the ice he was sitting on began spinning in the whirlpool. Ben realized something wasn't right, so he straightened up and began trying to pull the raft out of the whirlpool, it spun faster and faster, he felt as if he were in a tornado, he was becoming dizzy and frightened, but fully expected the raft to get out of the current of the whirlpool and continue on downstream. When he realized that he was sinking into the whirlpool, he stood up and yelled to the others. All three quickly sat up. They saw Ben standing on his piece of ice, spinning in circles, extremely fast. Lacey panicked, "JUMP!" she yelled.

Ben jumped from his twirling, sinking piece of ice and grabbed onto Lacey's outstretched arm. Relief washed over his face, but then as he looked at Trent, Megan, and Lacey's faces he realized something was wrong. He clung to Lacey's arm, but looked over his shoulder, the lower half of his body was being pulled under the water into the whirlpool. Trent and Megan began paddling, trying to pull him out of the whirlpool, but weren't strong enough. Ben felt his waist then his stomach go under the water. Soon it was his chest, and shoulders, one second later his head was under the water, which swirled ferociously around him. He held tight to Lacey's arm, thinking for sure she could pull him up and out of this nightmare. He held his breath and opened his eyes, just in time to see a blurry vision of Lacey floating in front of him, still clutched to his arm, Trent seemed to fly by them and quickly sank faster under the water in the spinning whirlpool, followed by Megan. Her strawberry blonde hair floated weightlessly around her face, her expression was one of an underwater scream, she clutched her chest with one hand and grasped the empty water with the other. Ben kicked and pulled Lacey trying to get down and closer to Megan as she sank deeper and deeper below them. With every pull toward Megan she seemed to be being pulled even faster away from him. The force of the water was too strong and he wasn't fast enough. He tried harder, pulled Lacey faster, his fingers touched Megan's as she struggled to grab his hand, right as their fingers touched an invisible force in the water yanked her away and she disappeared into the abyss below.

23

Megan's eyes and body ached, she was frozen, she pulled off her gloves and looked at her hands, they were dry at least, but blue and grey in color. She knew this couldn't be good, although she hurt she forced herself to stand up in the water. The tunnel she had gotten pulled down into spit her up into a small cave, the water was only a few feet deep and appeared to flow into another underwater tunnel about five feet from her.

The ceiling of the cave was rounded ice. She was in what she thought must be an air pocket that somehow hadn't collapsed. She waded around in the frigid water, looking for any escape. She certainly couldn't fight the current and go back the way she came in, the water was far too powerful. This left her only one other choice. She slowly and carefully walked to the other side of the cave, where the water appeared to be flowing. There was a tunnel on this side, she knelt down and looked at the space. At the top of the rounded tunnel, there was almost six inches of air space above the water flow.

"Well, I guess I have no other choice," she mumbled to herself and almost jumped as her voice echoed in the small cave. "Echo!" She shouted and listened to her voice ricochet off the blue icy walls. She smiled and took a deep breath, knowing she would need it to tolerate submerging herself into the cold water again. She sat carefully at the entrance to the tunnel. The cold water filled her coat and pants once again, she squealed from the pain, but then quickly decided it wouldn't do any good, so she bit her tongue and got ready for what could be her last breath.

She reached up to the top of the tunnel and casually pushed herself in, as if she were simply entering a water slide at an amusement park. It quickly became dark inside the tunnel, she kept her face above the water and tried to convince her body to just float, it became harder and harder though, she was so nervous, her legs kept instinctively going down trying to get footing on the icy floor. The water had carved a smooth surface, and so finally as she grew tired, she let her legs relax, her boots scratched along the bottom, working to slow her down at least, until finally there was no bottom and she was falling once again.

⁂

Ben's head throbbed, he found his temple with his gloved hand and began massaging it before he opened his eyes. As he gained more and more consciousness, he slowly managed to open his eyes, what he saw didn't make much sense. He focused in on the circular object more, trying to make sense of what appeared to be an enormous eyeball encased in ice.

He closed his eyes once again and this time moved his head back a bit to get a better look. As he did, he realized he was looking at an enormous eyeball, he gasped and tried to stand, slipping on the ice he slammed against the icy wall and found himself face to face with a huge Wooly Mammoth. It's body was perfectly frozen in the glacier's ice. It's brown fur and thick hairy trunk looked as though it had happened just days before. The clarity was profound. Ben followed the beast's legs, and back, he stepped back trying to take in the entire magnificence of the animal when all the sudden he tripped over something, and then landed hard on his back and cracked his head against the icy floor.

"Ouch." Lacey moaned. She looked around and screamed as the vision of the Wooly Mammoth stared her straight in the face.

In terror, she rolled over and met Ben's knee, which slammed her in the eye.

She grabbed her eye and moaned again, then asked, "You okay Ben?"

"My head is killing me."

"Yeah, mine too." She sat next to him and looked around. The sound of splashing water brought her attention to what must have been their entry point into the cavern they sat in. Once again, they were surrounded by ice, the water from the river lapped against the icy beach in which they sat. It was like a frozen lagoon, the blue ice shone brightly, the crystal clear water flowed past them and around a bend leading to what Lacey imagined to be only one thing...more ice.

Suddenly it hit Lacey, "Oh my gosh, where's Megan? Where's Trent?" she yelled. She jumped to her feet then slipped and caught herself on something that was protruding from the ice behind her. She looked down and saw her hand wrapped around what appeared to be a long, dark brown horn. She followed the horn, it went back into the ice and met the Wooly Mammoth's face, it wasn't a horn at all she realized, it was an enormous tusk. She let it go quickly, almost as if she were in a museum and someone was going to tell her to let go of such an ancient artifact.

Ben gasped as he stood up and headed to the side of the cave where the river disappeared around the corner. Lacey followed not knowing what to make of her nephew's actions. Ben jumped back into the water and started to swim to whatever he saw, he grabbed onto something, Lacey was too far away to see exactly what it was until Ben pulled the object closer to him. It was Trent, he was floating lifelessly in the freezing water, face down. Lacey screamed when she saw his lifeless body, Ben pushed Trent toward Lacey, she grabbed his arm and began pulling him onto the bank. As they slid him up and rolled him over, his still glassy eyes made Lacey shiver.

Lacey unzipped his jacket and began pounding on his chest, she stopped momentarily and listened for his heart, not hearing anything, she began again. Ben put his hands on each side of Trent's face and rolled his head to the side, hoping maybe this would help any water come out, "Give him mouth to mouth!" Lacey yelled at Ben.

"What? Mouth to mouth...uh...I...uh," he stalled looking at Trent's lifeless face, "Lacey I don't know how to do that and...and...*EWW!*" Lacey pushed Ben to the side,

"Fine, you do the heart compressions, I'll do it!" With that she plugged Trent's nose then lowered her mouth to Trent's and began blowing air into his lungs. Ben continued to push in on Trent's ribs, Lacey continued to blow air into his lungs, they paused only for a second or two at a time to listen and see if there was any sign of life.

Just as Lacey lowered her face back to Trent's a low gurgling sound escaped his lips, followed by an enormous wave of projectile vomit. Lacey screamed and threw her face back as it covered her, she was dripping with a mixture of water and whatever Trent had eaten for lunch. She wiped her face and her mouth with her hands. It was in her eyes, her hair, even her ears. She opened her eyes and saw Trent shaking and throwing up even more. Ben had rolled him onto his side, and was holding his head as his whole body convulsed with every heave.

Finally the heaving stopped, Trent wiped his mouth and looked up to the vomit covered Lacey,

"Oh no, I'm...I'm so sorry," he whispered. He was too exhausted to say anything else, he reached over and grabbed Lacey's hand, "Thank you."

Lacey just sat there as he caught his breath, Ben couldn't help but laugh, he was so relieved that Trent was alive and well the fact that his aunt was covered in vomit was just too much. He grabbed Trent below the arms and lifted him to a sitting position.

Trent's head hung low and he looked up to Lacey with huge embarrassed eyes, "I'm so sorry I threw up all over you, I uh never thought that would be how our first uh…" he got quiet suddenly.

"What?" Lacey questioned, her eyes wide, and her cheeks blushing.

Ben looked at both of them, embarrassment overcoming him and yelled, "*AND CUT!*" just as a movie director would if something wasn't going quite right. "Let's just save this for another time, huh, guys…yeah? Let's get out of here and then you can get all mushy, if not you're gonna make me vomit." He laughed then helped Trent to his feet.

Lacey knelt down to the frigid water and took handfuls to clean her face and hair, she shuttered from the cold. As she stood, Trent looked at her and mouthed the words, 'I'm sorry.'

She smiled and grabbed his hand, "I'm so glad you're okay." They stared at each other for a few seconds too long.

Ben said, "Really? Really guys? Can we at least try to get out of here and find Megan, sheesh!" He stepped into the water and began walking down the tunnel where the river proceeded.

"Megan's gone?" Trent asked.

"She's gotta be somewhere, we'll find her," Lacey said trying to convince herself.

The beach ended as the water disappeared into another tunnel. Lacey and Trent followed Ben and all three were forced to lie back in the water and float in the darkness. They each held on to the boot of the person behind them to make sure they didn't get separated, the flow of the water began to increase, the current was powerful as the tunnel got more and more narrow. Ben held his head up above the water's surface to look ahead in the tunnel, hoping he would see Megan, what he saw instead was a circular bright blue patch of sky.

"Guys there's sky up ahead, I think the tunnel is ending!" Just as Trent and Lacey lifted their heads to see their exit, the current became incredibly forceful, and a pounding, rushing sound vibrated the walls around them. Ben realized what was happening before Trent and Lacey could articulate it, he screamed, "WATERFALL!"

The three held each other's boots tighter as Ben went over the edge of the waterfall, and out of the glacier. His falling pulled on Trent and then of course Lacey, they fell only a few feet, but each screamed along the way, not knowing how high this waterfall really was. As they hit another body of water, each relaxed as they realized they were indeed alive. Ben pulled himself to the surface and was almost blinded by the bright sunlight shining on him. The fresh air filled his lungs and he rejoiced that he could see trees and mountains and someone running into the water nearby him, he focused on the person but before he could yell out her name, Megan was almost pushing him under the water she was hugging him so hard. Trent and Lacey had come to the surface as they realized what was going on. They swam over to Ben and Megan and began hugging each other too, everyone relaxed a bit as they were bear hugging Megan.

Quietly Megan said, "So, yeah…it's cold." She looked at them all, clearly thankful they were alive and then repeated, "No really guys, I was warming up on the beach, it's cold in here!" They all laughed, Ben grabbed Megan's shoulders and dunked her under the water, as she emerged she punched him in the arm, she wiped her hair from her face then said seriously, "Now that's just rude, Ben."

24

"Thanks again, for the lift." Trent shook the hand of each snow mobile driver then walked over to Lacey, toward the plane which was still waiting on the glacier.

"Hurry, let's check on Compass!" Megan demanded as she jogged over to the door. Trent opened the small door for her and there still tucked inside a warm blanket, resting on top of a hot water bottle was the small wolf pup, sound asleep. She gently scooped him up in her arms and held him to her neck. He nuzzled her softly and then began rooting around her neck, an indication that he was clearly hungry.

Megan climbed in the plane and retrieved a small baby bottle that contained the powdered milk Sarah had given her to feed Compass with. She emptied some of the warm water from the hot water bottle into the baby bottle and mixed up the formula, then laid Compass on her lap as he suckled the warm milk.

"Looks like you've got that down," Lacey acknowledged as she climbed in the seat next to Megan.

"Yeah, I love this lil' guy." Megan beamed.

Trent and Ben tossed a black garbage bag that was full of their wet clothes behind the seat, then climbed in the front and started the engine.

"Good thing the people at the information center at the lake had extra clothes, we'd have frozen to death." Megan said as she stroked Compass' forehead.

"Yeah, that was very cool, I imagine quite a few people need spare clothes after trekking on the glacier, or falling into the lake like we did, amazing though, I never knew that Mendenhall Lake even existed, I thought all glaciers ended at the ocean for some reason. That place was amazing." Lacey yawned as she spoke, then quickly closed her eyes.

"You guys ready?" Trent called back to them over the humming of the engine and the vibration of the propellers.

"As ready as we'll ever be!" Megan called back.

Trent initiated take off and within a minute they were flying over the mountains and seeing the enormous glacier from the sky, it stretched for what appeared to be miles, Ben couldn't help but feel relieved knowing that Henry and Eddy were buried in it.

"So, I figure we'll head back to the hotel, see your parents, dry our clothes, get some supplies and head to the next waypoint." Trent said to Ben.

"How many supplies do you think we'll need? According to the areal maps it looks like the next geocache is only a few miles up the West Buttress trail on Mt. McKinley."

"Ben, people train for years to climb that mountain, what looks like only a few miles, could take days. If there is a storm, maybe weeks. We'll need to stock up, get some tents, heaters, climbing gear, this is gonna be intense. I'll fly us in as far as I can, but after that it's up to us and mother nature."

"I have a feeling we'll be okay," Ben said, totally at peace. He wasn't sure what was causing his overall calm. Perhaps it was that they had faced death time and time again. Maybe it was that he was sensing an end to this journey. Or maybe it was the fact that he knew they weren't alone. Something, some force was protecting them, he was finally allowing that thought to take precedence over his fear.

"Oh yeah, I'm sure we will, besides if it gets too dangerous there's no harm in quitting" Trent said as he adjusted some gauges.

"I don't think that'll happen," Ben replied.

"Why?" Trent asked.

"Every time we've tried to quit something happens, I think... I think there is a greater purpose in us following this Cache Master, I think..." he paused not knowing if he sounded silly or not, then decided he didn't care, "I think it's fate."

"Huh?" Trent thought on what Ben had said and then added, "Well I believe in fate, I think you're right, I think it was my fate to meet you guys, especially your aunt."

"Oh boy, here we go." Ben laughed. Trent looked behind him and saw Lacey sleeping on Megan's shoulder, he was relieved she hadn't heard him. He turned his eyes back to the clouds in front of him and settled in for the flight.

Lacey kept her eyes closed but couldn't stop the big smile that had appeared on her blushing face. She suddenly, for the first time in her life, was starting to believe in fate too.

☙❧

There was no end to the sunlight here, for a few hours it would get a little darker, but never totally dark, it was confusing to the body and mind. As Trent and Lacey loaded the plane with climbing gear Ben and Megan hugged their parents and got ready for their journey.

The flight to Mt. McKinley wasn't long, but by the time they arrived it felt as though only minutes had passed. Although adrenaline was playing a huge part, there was also a sense of relief. Ben and Megan had agreed with their parents that regardless of what this geocache held, this would be their last stop. After this one, they would go back to Anchorage and fly out, in exactly five days.

Once they had landed, secured the plane, and gotten loaded up with their packs, which held the tent, food rations, hiking and climbing gear and in Megan's case a very tiny wolf pup, the group began climbing the West Buttress trail. Even though it was June there was still plenty of snow, and the wind was relentless. They wound through the low lying forest, at the base of the mountain and slowly as they climbed in elevation the vegetation got more sparse and the snow changed into ice, much like the glacier they had just been on. It wasn't long before they had to tie their safety ropes together to hopefully prevent another fall into a crevasse. The stories Trent had told them about all the people who died, *who were experienced climbers*, made them take this very seriously.

The first day they made it two miles up the trail, before setting up camp and settling in for the night. The wind shook their tent, it was a scary feeling to know that between the elements and the four of them there was only a piece of fabric, but through laughter and conversation they somehow all dozed off to sleep, bundled in their sleeping bags like mummies.

The next day was very similar to the first, the climbing was slow, the weather was cold, windy, and scary. Sheets of glacier-like ice and snow, scarred with crevasses terrified the group. Sometimes putting one foot in front of the other took more courage and strength than they ever imagined. It was crazy how fear played such a huge part of this climb. They knew the fear wasn't helpful, but at the same time, they had to pay attention to every step, they had to know that at any minute one of the group members could fall into a crevasse and disappear, forever. The mental and emotional stress was almost worse than the physical stress on their bodies.

After a few hours of hiking the four explorers sat on the icy snow and opened up their MRE's they had purchased from a sporting goods store. These readymade meals; which were dehydrated foods, basically blended together. They were high calorie, high carbohydrate, high fat and highly disgusting. All they had to do was add water, and then somehow stomach swallowing the concoction without barfing. Ben quickly decided that was a task in itself. He coughed as he plugged his nose and tried to consume his mixture of food.

"You okay?" Trent asked, genuinely concerned that Ben may choke.

"Oh yeah, I'm just not used to liquefied roast beef. It's um delicious, do you wanna trade?" he coughed again trying to keep the food down.

"No, I'm good, I have scrambled eggs with bacon," Trent said sarcastically.

"This is awful!" Megan complained.

"Well, you whiney babies, we only have about three quarters of a mile, according to the GPS, let's just down this stuff, and get back to it, maybe we can get to the geocache and somehow make it back to the plane by tomorrow," Lacey said optimistically as she stood.

"Wait, wait…I just need a few more minutes, I'm gonna puke if I have to keep going right now, this food it's just…it's just," Ben covered his mouth in another attempt to keep his food in his stomach.

"I guess we can wait a little longer, they don't call it 'Buttress" for nothing," Lacey giggled.

"Well my *butt* definitely needs a *rest!*" Ben laughed then all the sudden couldn't control himself and threw up next to Lacey.

Lacey let out a scream as she leaned away from him, "What is it with you guys and vomiting either on me or next to me, it's just not fair!" She whined.

"Sorry," Ben said as he wiped his mouth and nose, "At least it was pureed, I guess."

"Okay gross, Ben!" Megan yelled and kicked snow at him.

Trent handed Ben a bottle of water and an energy bar, "Try this for now, and Lacey, well at least he didn't get you in the face," Trent laughed.

Lacey made a gagging sound then stood quickly, "Seriously just being by it is making me sick, let's go you guys, then we don't have to look at it, yuck Ben...*really*, you couldn't aim *away* from the group?!"

"Like Trent said, at least I didn't aim toward your face," Ben smiled and giggled to himself, then climbed onto his feet and helped Megan up.

The group worked slowly on the trail, through valleys of ice and hills which they had to zigzag along switchbacks in order to safely gain altitude, the journey was tedious, but just as they were all becoming exhausted Lacey announced that they were within one hundred feet of the geocache according to the GPS on her phone.

They all paused and looked around, for anything that may have a geocache attached to it, as they glanced about the icy landscape they all settled in on one thing, a large bright yellow sign which read "HAZARD AVALANCHE ZONE."

"Okay everyone, let's move slow and let's be quiet, we really, really, really don't wanna test our avalanche survival skills today." Trent said. The group worked slowly to the sign, then once at the location, they began looking around it. The phone had indicated that this was the spot, and the GPS accuracy rating was within five feet so they knew that if the geocache was here it would be attached to this sign.

Finding nothing on the sign, Ben got out his ice pick and began gently digging and chipping away ice and snow that surrounded the post which was holding the sign up.

"Please be careful!" Trent warned quietly.

"Don't worry, I will, I just figure this post has to be pretty tall, the snow level must change a lot here." He continued to break small pieces of ice away and uncovered more and more of the frozen wooden post. Once he had cleared almost two feet of snow from the post, his pick hit something metal, he looked at everyone, excitement overcoming him, then dug more quickly.

"Please, Ben, slow down." Trent cautioned again. Ben took his advice and slowed down, but quickly uncovered the box, it was attached to the post, they couldn't remove it, so Ben was forced to lay on his stomach and unlock the box within the small hole he had dug. As he twisted the key everyone held their breath, as he opened the lid and another brass key fell out, everyone sighed in disappointment.

"Seriously?!" Megan shouted with frustration, just as she did a large cracking sound echoed around the group. Her eyes became wide with fear and regret, they all grabbed each other's hands, knowing what was about to happen. As the first wave of snow moved under their feet Trent pulled them all down into a crouching position, he grabbed onto the HAZARD sign and held tight, as the snow plowed over the top of them, burying each one in an icy tomb.

25

The thick frozen wood post from the hazard sign laid heavy across Trent's back. He felt as though a tree had fallen on top of him, rather than just a six inch post. Trent moved his shoulders a bit, and then managed to free one hand to wipe the snow and ice from his eyes and face. He held tight to Lacey who had grabbed his other hand right before the avalanche had buried them.

As he shifted his weight he realized that they weren't buried completely in snow, the post of the hazard sign had snapped, pushing the large sign on top of them, creating a barrier of sorts. As he used all his strength to lift the sign, which was covered in loose powder, he thought about the irony of the situation, the sign which warned them, had also saved them.

As Trent lifted the sign, Lacey, Ben, and Megan began to slowly move and assess their injuries. They each climbed out of the snow, which was now chest deep, with moans and cries of pain and fear.

"I'm so sorry," Megan whispered, for fear of causing another avalanche.

"It's okay, Megz, I'm just glad we're all okay," Ben hugged his sister gently, as he did he noticed movement under her thick coat, "Is Compass okay?"

"I think so, probably just a little scared, poor thing." She reached into her coat and pulled out the stunned small wolf pup. He nuzzled her neck and face, she gave him a quick kiss on the nose and then returned him to his warm sanctuary within her coat.

Trent laid the Hazard sign face down then sat on the back of it, using it for a seat. "Well guys, we have to get back, it's just too dangerous to stay up here. Let's try to get back to where we camped last night, before nightfall."

Lacey pulled her sleeve back and checked her watch, "Too late, it's already night." The group looked at the horizon, there was no sign of darkness, just a thick wall of clouds moving in and a swift wind blowing.

"Well, we'll probably get a few hours of darkness, so let's get a move on before we get stuck out here tonight." Trent stood up from his seat on the sign, then looked at it one more time, "Ya know, it's gonna be horrible to try to walk down the hill in this thick powder, probably dangerous too…we could probably fit two people on this sign and use it to slide down."

"What about the other two?" Ben asked.

Lacey threw him the safety rope and motioned for him to tie it onto the end of the broken post. "Two of us slide down, then the two on the slope pull the sign back up and slide down. We can do it in stages." She smiled at her quick thinking. "Megan and I will go first, then you and Trent can go." She motioned for Megan to sit on the front end of the sign, then climbed on behind her.

Once they were both stable enough, Trent put his hands on Lacey's back and pushed as hard as he could. The sign moved slowly at first but within seconds picked up speed. Both Lacey and Megan tried not to scream as they sailed down the side of the mountain, the wind and icy air biting at their faces. As the incline of the slope lessened, their speed did as well and suddenly the make shift sled lurched to a stop. The three hundred feet of rope had run out and Trent was holding on to the other end up on the mountainside.

Lacey and Megan rolled off the sign and lay on their stomachs across the snow. They weren't sure if there were crevasses under the new fresh snow which had fallen in the avalanche, so they decided it would be best to simply lay flat and distribute their weight until the guys made it down to them.

Trent and Ben both pulled and tugged on the rope until finally the now ice covered Hazard sign sat in front of them. Ben climbed on the front end, Trent gently climbed on behind him, then both used their gloved hands to push off. Again the sign moved slowly at first, but this time the icy sheet on the bottom made the sign slide much faster, within a second they were going so fast they couldn't stop. Lacey and Megan watched with their mouths wide open as Trent and Ben flew past them, cutting through the thick powder as if they were on a snowmobile. Both Trent and Ben had their hands over the sides trying to brake by digging into the snow, but there was no use.

Ben looked ahead and saw that within seconds they would fly over the edge of the snow covered cliff, "BAIL!" Ben yelled to Trent, both rolled off the high speed sign and landed in the soft powder, laughing. As Ben sat up covered in snow a strange noise caught his attention, it was the sound of something dragging, he couldn't quite place the noise until he felt the pull on his wrist. The safety rope which he had tied around his wrist had come to an end. Just as he felt the pain, there was a snapping noise as the rope popped then began dragging him. With his jacket and snow pants he sailed over the top of the snow just as easily as the sign had. The snow was bunching up under his chin as he skinned his entire face with lumps of ice and debris. He screamed in pain and tried to untie his wrist, but couldn't get enough grip on the rope to unloop it. As he was being dragged he decided to try to roll onto his back, he flipped over just as the sign went over the cliff, then suddenly felt weightless as he also flew over the edge of the cliff.

The weightless feeling only lasted a split second before he felt himself free-falling, being pulled by the weight of the falling sign. He called out for help, knowing no one would hear him and that they had no way of getting to him. Finally, he hit the soft snow covered ground and came to a stop. His body ached, and he checked himself for any injuries. He wiped his face and realized he was bleeding from scraping along the snow for so long. Trying to alleviate the pain he took handfuls of snow and pressed them to his stinging skin. Ben shrieked in pain as the stinging only got worse, but soon relief came as numbness took over.

Once he had enough strength, he turned and looked at the cliff behind him, it was probably about four hundred feet high, he guessed. He squinted as he looked up trying to spot, Megan, Trent or Lacey, he saw no one and so he stood and wandered a little ways from the cliff side so he could get a better line of sight to the top. Once he was about fifty feet out from the base of the cliff, he saw that Megan, Trent, and Lacey were all standing at the top, waving and calling out to him. Ben waved back trying to show them all that he was okay, not realizing that the main thing they could see was the bright red blood stained snow that scarred the pristine white surface.

Not knowing what else to do, since he couldn't exactly yell to them for fear of causing yet another avalanche, Ben took the safety rope and dragged it across the surface, laying it out in the shape of an arrow. From this level he could see that the slope they were on continued down until intersecting with the level he was on about a mile to the east. Ben made the arrow and then waited for them to understand what he was trying to say.

Once Trent, Lacey, and Megan began moving in the direction of the arrow Ben untied the safety rope and rolled it up. He stuffed it in his pack then started the slow hike to where the slopes intersected.

Ben's pathway was quickly being taken over by forest, the shrubs and trees first slowly crept into his path and then became denser the lower in altitude he was. The snow was thick around the bases of the trees, and unstable, he worked his way slowly through the thicket of trees, grabbing onto branches and bushes as he walked by.

A few minutes into his struggle through the snowy forest he grabbed onto what he thought was a branch, but its denseness felt different, it was bone-like to the touch. He quickly looked more closely and saw that what he was actually holding onto was the tip of an antler. He let go quickly and then saw that the antler was protruding from a large fresh mound of snow. Ben began removing the snow from the antlers, uncovering a huge bowl like shape, that was thick and solid, as he dug more and more he uncovered both sides of the antlers and realized he was next to an enormous moose.

Its body was still covered in snow, Ben felt sorry for the animal, he assumed it was eating or something innocent when the avalanche came over the edge of the cliff and clobbered the poor thing. He continued to hold onto the thick antlers, looking at their sheer size and becoming more and more curious about the beast that could haul these things around. The rack was at least five feet wide and probably weighed at least one hundred pounds, if not more.

Ben began to dig more and more, he really wanted to get a good look at this moose, as he did he kept sinking into the snow and so he made a fateful decision and climbed onto the antlers.

They were so thick he knew they would support him and disperse his weight so he could really focus on simply unburying this huge animal.

He kneeled on the bulky antlers and began to sweep the snow away from what he assumed to be the face of the moose, he uncovered an ear and got even more excited, then dug faster and faster, it was when he uncovered the forehead and the eyes that he knew he was in trouble. Just as he brushed the snow from the beast's face it opened its eyes, made a strange coughing, moaning, groaning sound.

Ben's eyes grew wide, he turned and tried to jump off the antlers just as the moose rolled and pulled itself up in the snow. His body lifted so fast all he could do was hold on, suddenly he was over seven feet in the air. The angry and stunned moose shook his head fiercely. Ben gripped the antlers more tightly as he was being thrown from side to side. Ben perched himself into a crouch and was going to jump off just as the moose began running. Ben yelled out in fear and then pain as branch after branch slapped him in the head and shoulders. All he could do was lower his head to his chest trying to protect himself, as this confused beast barreled through the forest. The animal was literally running right over the top of ten foot tall trees, not even attempting to dodge them, Ben turned around thinking he would have better protection from the branches and looked backwards behind the frantic animal. As it continued to hurl itself full speed through the forest, Ben steadied himself and decided now was the time to jump off. If he did it quickly enough the moose may not notice and may be too scared to turn on him and attack him.

Ben lifted himself up, getting whacked in the head by more branches as he did, he was just about to leap when he noticed three huge grey objects following, no, *chasing* the moose. The pack of wolves came closer and closer to the moose's hind quarters, they nipped and growled as they leapt trying to grab onto one of the moose's legs. Ben turned toward the front, a huge thick branch was only feet from his head, as the moose barreled through the trees it occurred to him, whether he hit the branch, or jumped to the wolves…he was dead, either way.

26

Trent held tightly to Lacey and Megan's hands as they eased themselves off of the icy ledge and onto the flat rocky ground below. Once steadied, they all began to look around for Ben, they thought for sure he would be waiting for them at this point, it was the most obvious intersection point of the two areas.

As they all peered into the thick forest, Compass began clawing Megan wildly. She squealed in pain as his tiny little claws began climbing up her chest. She jumped and wiggled and tried to break him free from her skin, finally she managed to unzip her coat and pull him out.

The tiny wolf pup was going crazy thrashing around and attempting to howl, but all that came out was a tiny quiet whine. Megan paced around trying to get him to settle down, finally, she couldn't hold onto him and she accidently dropped him onto the snow covered ground. The pup instantly began wobbling and wandering toward the forest. Trent and Lacey quickly caught up as Megan followed the pup into the woods.

꩜

Ben decided his best chance for survival would be to stay on the moose. With his blood covered face he was sure that if he attempted to grab onto the branch, the wolves would be more attracted to him and stay at the base of the tree until they could somehow manage to pull Ben to the ground.

He quickly lowered himself and just barely missed the large branch, it grazed him along the top of his head and back, causing him to holler out in pain. Just as his cry stopped he was dropping through the air. He wasn't sure what had happened, but suddenly the moose fell to the ground. He panicked thinking the wolves had finally brought the animal down. As he opened his eyes though, he realized he heard something, something faint and tiny. In this moment he also realized he didn't hear something else. He turned around wondering why the pack of wolves were suddenly quiet, had they given up?

Looking back only three or four feet from the tail end of the moose the three large wolves lay on the ground cowering, small wines came out of their muzzles, long gone were the ferocious flesh tearing growls that had haunted him the last several minutes.

Ben turned again trying to find the source of the small howl he heard, he looked through the forest, through the dense branches and bushes and in the distance he saw three figures coming toward him. Imagining what could make a moose and three huge wolves cower brought him almost to tears. He hunkered down closer to the moose in an effort to try to protect himself, as the footsteps got closer and the howl became louder he realized that he recognized it.

Ben looked up and saw Megan following the tiny wolf pup, who continued to howl with all its might, finally the pup stopped and stood with its feet wide apart, and the gruff on its neck standing up, as it would if it had been an adult wolf showing its dominance by making all of its fur stand on end.

"Megan?" Ben whispered. Megan bent over and picked Compass up, as she did he howled louder and louder, with each howl the wolves and the moose lowered their heads more and more. Ben looked around completely stunned by what was happening. He climbed off the moose' antlers and carefully started backing away from the animals. As he did, he tripped and stumbled backwards, falling onto his rear end. Suddenly one of the large wolves jumped up, thinking perhaps that it could make its move and finally attack the blood covered boy. Just as the wolf made its move Compass howled again, as he did, the other two wolves jumped up and attacked the wolf that had moved toward Ben. They fought for a second, and as Compass howled again all three whimpered and laid down, this time rolling onto their backs to show their true submission.

Trent and Lacey moved toward Ben and pulled him to his feet, he was shaking and terrified. They moved behind Megan and Compass, once all three were behind Megan, Compass let out a quick small bark. All of the sudden the wolves jumped up and turned, tails between their legs and ran as fast as they could back into the thick forest. The moose waited for a moment, then it stood also. Ben watched its massive body rise before them. The moose took a few steps toward Megan, who was standing tall and strong. Compass wiggled in Megan's hand, until she outstretched it to the moose. He lowered his large head, toward Megan's hand. The beast's face was almost a foot wide and a few feet long, the heavy antlers sat on top defying gravity. The moose took a humble step forward and touched its muzzle to Compass' muzzle. The small wolf pup licked the moose's nose a few times, then turned toward Megan.

The moose backed away from Megan and Compass, then turned its enormous body around and galloped off into the forest in the opposite direction that the wolves had retreated to. Once he had disappeared Compass began nuzzling Megan's arm, she brought him to her face and neck, he licked her a few times, then began to root down into her coat once again. She turned to Ben, Trent, and Lacey who were standing in awe behind her.

Megan paused, then looked thoughtfully at the group, "*So, so RANDOM!*"

Ben smiled, everything was beginning to make sense, "Not really Megz, it's just like Katie said, 'sometimes the tiniest voice is the most commanding.'"

27

Ben and Megan's mom ran out on the tarmac and practically knocked them over with a huge bear hug, "I heard about the avalanche, I was terrified! This is OVER now! I'm sorry, but the answer is no, this is OVER!" she squeezed them tighter.

"Mom..." Ben wrestled away from her, "Mom I have this key though, and well the GPS says it's in Anchorage, could we just go to it? Why don't you guys just come with us?"

Ben's dad looked at his mom, "Honey, why not? We've never been geocaching anyways, might be fun to see what it's all about?" He smiled at Ben and Megan, knowing he had just won huge points with them.

Ben's mom paused, "It's really here? Like in town or what?"

"Well yeah, it looks like it is, the aerial map shows a city street..." Ben looked to his aunt for help.

"Yeah sis, come with us, then as soon as we're done you guys can head home."

※

Ben, Megan, their parents, Lacey, and Trent stood outside the tall doorway of the Anchorage Community Credit Union. The glass doors reflected their image and Ben couldn't help but think of how they must look, a family, that had been through the wringer, stalking the outside of a bank. They had searched the street, the sign posts, the benches, even garbage cans for the geocache and found nothing. The actual waypoint pointed to what should be inside the building, he was worried that at any minute security guards would appear and arrest them for loitering, or for planning a bank heist.

"Well if the GPS says it's inside, shouldn't we just go in?" Ben's mom asked.

"Well, yeah, but what exactly are we gonna do, it's not like we can look around inside for the geocache, right?" Megan said in a defeated tone. She'd had enough of this journey, it was fun, it was crazy and definitely exciting, but she was tired and really wanted to get back to her swimming pool and introduce Compass to her older dog, Nicolas.

Ben interrupted her thoughts and said, "Ya know what, maybe it's inside, look…" he handed the key to Lacey, "I was so focused on the waypoint, I didn't even notice the letters on the back of the key."

Lacey turned the key over in her hand and saw the letters "ACCU" inscribed in the brass. "I wonder if we go in and show one of the tellers the key, maybe they can help us, it's worth a shot, right?" With that, she opened the large heavy door and walked right up to the counter.

There was a small lobby, with a few leather chairs, a table made of antlers and glass held magazines, and a small flat screen TV played the local news. Ben's dad and mom sat in the chairs and waited.

Lacey, Trent, Megan, and Ben waited at the counter for the teller to get off the phone. The young woman had long brown hair and smiled nervously at the group, not quite understanding why they were all standing so closely, most people who were tending to their banking, preferred privacy.

"Can I help you guys?" she asked nicely enough.

Lacey lifted up the key and handed it to the teller, "This is gonna sound crazy, but we're geocaching, and well in this last geocache was this key, and the waypoint leads here, and it has the banks initials on the back, and well..." she paused waiting for some sort of response from the teller who was examining the key, "Well, do you know what it goes to, or if we're in the right place?"

The teller smiled brightly and replied, "Uh...just a second, let me get my manager." She quickly walked away from the counter and knocked on a door to the left with a large gold colored name plate that read, "BRANCH MANAGER." Ben and Megan watched as she handed the key to the man sitting behind a large desk inside the office, he looked at the key, his eyes got large and he quickly stood up and rushed out of the office.

"So, you guys say you *found* this in a geocache?" he asked with one eyebrow raised.

"Yes, sir." Ben replied, nervously.

"Well, okay..." he shook his head and wiped his forehead, then smiled at each of them, "I've been waiting for this key to come in!" He seemed anxious for some reason. "This key goes to a safety deposit box, but you need to have the Password to get full access."

"Password, we don't have a Password, only the key," Lacey interrupted.

"No, I know, the Password is a question that you have to answer, just so I know that you came by the key honestly."

Lacey looked nervously at the rest of the group, "Okay, what's the question?" the man ran back to his office, used the key to open a drawer on his desk and pulled out a manila envelope, he had it opened by the time he was back to the counter.

"Okay, the question is...'Who sent you here?'" He tapped his nails on the counter as he waited for a response.

"Uh...well it wasn't a 'who' it was just in the geocache..." Ben responded.

"No, no Ben..." Megan interrupted him, "The Cache Master sent us here, he's the one who placed the geocaches, right?" She looked expectantly at the manager.

"Yes, you're right. Okay guys, follow me!" He walked around the counter and headed toward a door that read "Safety Deposit Boxes" He unlocked the thick metal door, then handed the key back to Lacey, "You have a key and I have a key." He said as he slipped a second key out of the manila envelope. The group followed the manager past rows and rows of safety deposit boxes, Megan felt as though she were in a high security post office, with how the boxes were stacked and numbered on top of one another.

The manager paused at a box, turned and said, "Here it is, we'll both use our keys, then you can take it to the table at the end of the room," he motioned to a large metal table along the far wall of the vault, "and you can see what's inside."

Both he and Lacey inserted their keys and turned them, the locks popped opened and the manager swung open the small door, revealing a small, metal box about the size of a laptop. He pulled the box out and placed it in Megan's hands, "I'll leave you to it, when you're done, just let me know." He smiled broadly and walked back to the heavy vault door, as soon as he exited the room the group ran over to the table and gently set the box down.

Everyone looked at each other, not sure what they were going to find, but excited that this geocache seemed to be extra special to the Cache Master. Ben couldn't wait, he lifted the lid to the box, inside was another manila envelope. He picked it up and felt around, feeling nothing strange he gently tore open the end of the envelope, then held it upside down, the contents slipped out onto the metal table.

There was a brass key, which Megan instantly grabbed, Ben picked up a plastic folder that contained a torn piece of old aged paper inside, and Lacey and Trent grabbed a small stack of papers and began reading them, Lacey cleared her throat, "Okay guys, this is someone's Will."

"Will? Like someone left something for us when they died?" Megan asked.

"It says, 'This is the last Will and Testament of Roy Morgan, whom ever has accessed this is the current beneficiary by Alaska state law to the contents of this Safety Deposit Box," Lacey scanned the document looking for more information, then added, "Okay it says here in the 'personal messages to heirs' section: Thank you for playing my game, if you wish to continue your prize will be grand, I trust that anyone who can make it this far has the strength and courage to make the ultimate decision for the final prize.'" Lacey looked at the other contents, "Megan, what do you have?"

"Another key, but the waypoint on it is really different from what we've been following, I don't think it's around here."

Lacey looked at Ben who's eyes were wide with amazement, "What about you, Ben?"

Ben turned the plastic folder over and held it up for everyone to see, "I…I think I have half of a deed to somewhere, like a piece of land?" He handed the folder to Trent who looked more closely at it.

After a few seconds Trent's jaw dropped, "this…this…" he shook it in his hands excitedly, "Okay guys, do you remember what I told you about the Pebble Beach Mine?"

"Yeah, about the gold? But we went there, there was nothing there." Ben said curiously.

"Not yet." Trent replied. He held the folder up, "You guys, this is half the deed to that land, if you find the other half of this…the land is yours. Which means the gold mine is yours too!" He handed the folder to Lacey. Lacey looked at Ben and Megan,

"How much gold did you say was in that mine again, Trent?" She stared wide eyed at him.

He shook his head almost unable to articulate the answer, then finally said, "Two hundred billion dollars."

28

Lacey hugged Megan at the end of the security line at the airport, "You sure you don't wanna fly home with us?" Megan asked for the tenth time.

Lacey held Trent's hand firmly, they looked at each other and smiled. "No Megz, I'm gonna stay up here for a while, someone's gotta get the RV, plus I need to look at the campus up here." Megan blushed when she saw Trent kiss the top of Lacey's head.

Ben's mom pulled her sister aside, "Lacey, you sure about this?"

"Of course." Lacey replied.

"Okay, but really, you're gonna switch colleges? I mean it's *really* cold up here!"

"Yeah, but I *really* like it up here." She smiled and then nodded toward Trent who was shaking Ben's dad's hand. "Plus, it's not like we aren't gonna see each other in a month." She held up the small brass key.

"True, and thank-you Cache Master for choosing someplace *warm* this time!" Ben's mom laughed. "I can so do Hawaii!" She giggled again.

"Yeah leave all the hard, dangerous geocaches to us." Lacey joked, "I see how you are, you'll only do tropical places," she nudged her sister, then leaned in and gave her a huge hug.

"Thank you for keeping my kids alive." Ben's mom whispered in Lacey's ear.

"Of course, I mean c'mon I don't think I could handle *that* lecture if something happened to them." She winked at her sister.

Ben's dad grabbed his mom's hand and pulled her into the line at security. Lacey gave everyone goodbye hugs then turned, grabbed Trent's hand and began walking away.

☙❧

The flight home seemed quick, it helped that Ben and Megan instantly fell asleep as soon as they were in the air. They walked sleepily through the Medford International Airport in Southern Oregon. It was small so their walk to baggage claim was less than five minutes.

They waited for their luggage to fall down from the conveyor belt onto the circular belt; luckily they only had a few bags that they had retrieved off the RV the day before. Ben and Megan's dad loaded the bags onto a luggage cart and headed out the sliding doors and into the parking lot. They were all happy to be home, but still excited and nervous about their next trip. They quickly loaded the car, climbed in and were on their way home.

"Can I use your phone to text Lacey to let her know we made it home?" Ben asked Megan. She sleepily tossed her phone to Ben who began typing a message. As their car pulled into their driveway Ben noticed a large dark colored sedan park on the street in front of their house. "I wonder if it's someone from the cell phone company, wanting all our pics from the trip?" Ben said to no one in particular as he stepped out of the car. Everyone got out and headed toward the sedan. As the door opened and a tall man emerged from the driver's seat, Megan instantly froze in her tracks. Ben noticed his sister's hesitation and paused waiting for the man to turn around. Their parents continued to walk toward the vehicle.

"Mom, Dad, wait!" Megan called out. The man turned around and just as Megan suspected her worst nightmare had come true. She began crying as she watched a bandaged and beat up Henry raise a gun up and point it at her parents. They instantly froze and lifted their hands.

Ben shook as he typed a quick message to his aunt, "911… we have a major problem." He almost screamed when the phone vibrated in his hand, he tapped on the screen then read the text,

"Here 2." Was all it said.

THE END.

Made in the USA
Charleston, SC
02 December 2012